The Year They Ate
HORSE

BY

CAROL CHRISTIAN WEST

Matchstick Literary
1-888-306-8885
orders@matchliterary.com

ABOUT THE BOOK

It was 1932-33. The Russian Premier Joseph Stalin kept something he caused to happen that year a secret. He bribed reporters to speak of the "blossoming of the Ukraine." He provided these reporters with the best food, the finest living quarters and companions. So they only reported good news that they invented.

Whereas, when a boy returned home from his uncle's house in Kharkiv, the city, to his home on a farm in the Ukraine, he found devastation. Now he saw people dying, their grain taken for taxes, his whole village of Podolsk suffering.

The boy, Taras, and his sister, Luda, devise a plan. They and their horse, Viktor, face unbelievable danger.

ABOUT THE AUTHOR

I graduated from Meredith College in Raleigh,N.C., certified to teach either English or history. When we moved to Greenville, N.C. in late August, however, all those positions were filled. I took the State Merit Exam and qualified to become an Interviewer with Public Welfare Department. I became a social worker and continued in that career for 20+ years.

I took correspondence and continuing education courses from UNC and Duke in fiction on the side as I found myself becoming interested in creative writing of all sorts; journal, poetry, songs, short stories, and the novel. I took my last classes at the Institute of Children's Literature in Redding, Connecticut, finishing one novel in the graduate course.

Not surprisingly, I often write about the underdog and the less advantaged, about how facing adversity and crises in out lives can make us stronger.

CONTENTS

Chapter 1 Return Home 1

Chapter 2. No Letter 5

Chapter 3. Voluntary Sign-Up 9

Chapter 4. Unity and Progress? 13

Chapter 5. GONE 18

Chapter 6. The Secret 22

Chapter 7. Swamp Meeting 27

Chapter 8. Scavenging Grain 32

Chapter 9. The Lookout 37

Chapter 10. Fires and Nightmares 41

Chapter 11. Looking For Father Dimitri 45

Chapter 12. The Wrong Horse 51

Chapter 13. Brush Torches, Vadeem? 56

Chapter 14. The Fishing Trip 60

Chapter 15. Snakes and Snails 64

Chapter 16. Poets To Siberia 67

Chapter 17. The Railway Station 70

Chapter 18. "Shoot at Something" 74

Chapter 19. The Hunter 78

Chapter 20. Aftermath 83

Chapter 21. Nadiya's Fury 86
Chapter 22. The Women's Revolt 89
Chapter 23. Home Hospital 94
Chapter 24. The Hunt 97
Chapter 25. The Miller's Risk 99
Chapter 26. The Horse's Predicament 105
Chapter 27. For the Better Good 108
Chapter 28. A Stick, Not A Stone 114
Chapter 29. The River 120

Chapter 1 Return Home

Taras jumped down from the carriage and dropped his duffel bag. White dust swirled over his feet as he looked around. Where was Father or Grandfather? No one was here to meet him? He'd sent a letter to his mother saying he'd be back today at three. It was three-thirty. Puzzled, he walked to the windows of the Poldosk train station and looked in. Over at the back of the empty room he saw two men in dark uniforms talking to each other. Uniforms? Who were they?

When he stopped through the doorway of the station, the tallest one looked up.

"What are you doing here, boy?" he asked, walking toward him.

The soldier spoke Ukrainian with a Russian accent.

"Just returning from my uncle's house, sir."

"You should have stayed there, boy, shouldn't he, Boris?"

The other man raised his bushy eyebrows. "Very definitely. Of course, it depends on where your uncle lives. Where does he live, boy?"

"In Kharkiv, sir."

"Well, yes, you should have stayed there."

"Why, sir? It was time for me to return home."

"So many questions!" The tall one's knee-high black boots shone; the heels clicked together. Taras' stomach clenched. These were Russian soldiers, no question.

"Yes, child, you'll know soon enough. Get on home, now. Your father will want to know where you are." The older soldier raised his band in a wave.

Through the open door, he watched the carriage that had brought him here roll away, the horse's hooves clacking on the cobblestones. No trains had been available.

He picked up his bag and walked out into the sunshine. That would have made him feel better if he hadn't seen the fence that had been built across the road. It was new. It looked odd here at the railway station. Fences were to contain animals. He knew that well.

They owned a cow, a goat, a pig, and two horses at heir wheat farm. There were no animals here.

He heard steps and turned back. The tall soldier had followed him and was tapping his riding crop on his boot.

"In case you're wondering, the fence is to keep the locals from leaving." The soldier had read his mind.

"By the way, what do you have in your bag?" I need to inspect it. Step here."

Taras slowly handed the bag over to the younger soldier.

The soldier reached in and immediately captured the box of chocolates.

"Ah, here are some fine-looking chocolates. A present from your aunt, no doubt.

We'll have these. You can't bring food into Podoslsk, how good I discovered them. No one makes better chocolate than the Ukrainians.

"We don't need those, Fritz. Let the boy keep them. We're just supposed to keep real food from coming in." The older soldier had stepped outside.

"Well, then, I'll have all to myself if you don't want them." Fritz grinned." I haven't eaten since noon.

Real food kept out? Taras was afraid to ask what they meant.

Just then horses whinnied from the back lot.

"We better feed the horses is what we better do." Boris pointed back.

"Start walking home, boy. Too bad we can't loan you a horse, but ours bite Ukrainians, anyway. Get going," Fritz ordered.

What a bully, Taras thought.

As he began his long walk, he looked back at the sleek, black horses.

So beautiful. I know you would like me. I'd be good to you like I am to Viktor, my horse. That was the thought that picked up his pace. Toward home. Toward his family.

He'd been walking not quite an hour by his watch, getting hungry now. He gazed out on the honey-colored wheat fields on either side of him. He'd almost forgotten how beautiful they were. Against the horizon, he could see the purple Carpathian Mountains. Here, between the fields and the mountains, he could take in the blue green of the firs and willows near the river. He'd been so glad to leave for the year in the city with his aunt and uncle and cousins. He'd gotten tired of farm chores and wished for city living. But, living in the city, he'd missed home and pictured all of them, Luda, his younger sister; Maria . his mother; Serveig, his father; Vadeem, his older brother; and his grandparents; Ivan and Katrina. He wiped his eyes and quickened his step.

Just ahead he had to smile at a villager's goat sticking his head through the fence that surrounded their house's front garden plot. Every house in the village had a vegetable garden. His mother and grandmother always put up plenty in jars for the winter. Now the goat's legs had cleared the fence and were hanging over the top. His bleats didn't bring anyone, but the goat never gave up hope. Taras remembered that.

He glimpsed a stork nest on top of the church steeple on the next corner, his church. The big, gray bird gliding off the nest was a common sight in the Ukraine. They liked to build in high, prominent places. Taras personally felt the stork should have been the national bird instead of the nightingale.

A red and black flag flew at the church's front door. That was new. "Community Club," the sign on the door said. Well, fine! Father Dimitri had always said they needed activities for the youth, a place for them to go. That seemed like a good idea. If there were things for the youth to do, it might keep them out of trouble.

He switched his bag to his other hand. What had happened? Why had his father, or Vadeem, or his Grandfather not come and gotten him? That really baffled him.

He kicked a rock in front of him as he walked. Suddenly a commotion ahead startled him. More dust rose from the back of tall trees on the curve of the road. He heard yelling. A big harvesting machine moved around the bend toward him. Two soldiers in black uniforms drove it. Another man ran alongside the harvester. He was screaming at the soldiers.

Chapter 2. No Letter

The young man screaming at the soldiers was his brother! Taras called out, waving his hand, "Vadeem!"

His brother looked in his direction.

"Taras!" Cheering, Vadeem stormed toward him and scooped him up in his arms.

The soldiers kept on moving, driving a big harvester away, the dust making a screen behind them. What was going on?

"Are you home for good? Yes?" Vadeem spun around.

"I promise, I promise, I am. Now put me down!"

"Vadeem obeyed. "Well, you know I missed you, little brother!"

Taras threw a punch at Vadeem's shoulder. His brother rubbed it.

"Feel my muscles now; I'm not little anymore!" Taras pointed to his arm.

Vadeem squeezed Tara's arm muscles. "Well, brother, you aren't taller, but you hit like you are much stringer. Have you been boxing?"

"Yes, I have. With cousins Petra and Stephan. They wrestle, too."

"You didn't miss me, then." Vadeem pretended to look sad.

"Oh, yes, I did. They argued a lot. When they'd box or wrestle, sometimes I thought they'd kill each other. I bragged to them about you, Vadeem. You'd have beaten them easily.

"How many girlfriends have you had this year while I was gone? Two, three?"

"Two, Taras, nothing serious. Hey, the soldiers! Help me chase them! We have to get back our tools!"

"We can't take them by ourselves, Vadeem; they have guns."

"Well, now they have taken all our tools and did not pay for them. How will we harvest our wheat? We will be ruined!" Vadeem shook his fists in the air.

"We can get them back, can't we? They're ours. Are they borrowing them?"

"They're stealing them for the States to use on the collective farms! They're gone!"

Taras had a lot more questions, but now they were home. Home It looked so good to him. Nothing fancy, tin roof, stucco and wood, old lace curtains at the windows. Where his family was.

"Taras, Taras!" It was his mother, running toward him, crying and pushing long wisps of black hair back up into her bun.

Luda, his sister laughed and cheered. Her long black curls bounced as she jumped up and down.

His grandmother duck-waddled out the front dirt walk. She waved and blew kisses; her thick white hair blew in an unruly halo around her face.

"Thank God," she beathed, her little prayer warming his heart.

They swarmed around him, hugged him, kissed him. Questions came at him from all directions.

"How long did it take you to get here?" Was it fun living in the city? Did you have lots of chores? You are taller! Did you see a lot of sights? Was it hard?"

Taras laughed. "Hold on, wait a minute. Let me look at you. It's been so long. I missed you so much!"

As they reached the front door, they had to let go of each other to get inside. That was all right, too. That was what he remembered about his family. A lot of love.

"Everybody sit to the table. We'll talk. I'll make some tea." His mother wiped her face again and turned on the kettle.

Where were his father, his grandfather? Of course, they were working out in the fields. No, here they were coming in the back door from the barn.

"Taras, Taras!" Father swept him up in his arms, almost squashing him.

"Help!" Taras called out, laughing. His grandfather stumbled up to them and shouted, "My turn," and wrestled Taras away from his father, squeezing him.

Taras wondered if he would ever be as tall as they were.

Finally they released him, and all of then sat down at the table to talk, his mother pouring tea.

"I had a big box of chocolates for you all from Aunt Claudia. I'm so sorry. A soldier at the train station took them!"

A big fist slammed the table. Everyone jumped in his seat. His father resembled a storm brewing. It was no secret that Vadeem got his temper from Father.

"I'm sorry, Father; he went through my whole bag and look the the chocolates."

"Those robbers, the Russians, that's just like them, taking candy from a child!"

His father raked his hands through his brown hair."I'm sorry, Trans. I'm not angry at you.

I'm angry at the soldiers!"

Father and Grandfather wore very serious expressions.

"Did you get my letter saying I was coming home today at three? I thought you would come with the cart and Viktor to get me."

Grandfather exchanged glances with Father.

"We got no letter, Tara. We certainly would have been there. We've received no mail in a long time." As she spoke, his mother's hands roses as if surrendering.

"No mail? Did the postman quit?"

'No, dear, we think someone's screening our mail, reading it."

"Reading our mail?"

"It's called an occupation, Taras. The Russians rule the whole country now."

Grandfather's eyes were dark with anger.

Chapter 3. Voluntary Sign-Up

A welcome sound woke Taras.

"Taras, breakfast! Come on down. Let's all eat together."

He hadn't heard his mother's voice call him for a year. He hadn't heard the church bells ring, or the cows mooing, going to pasture, or his horse whinny in excitement to see him. He was really glad to be home.

His stomach growled loudly; he was so hungry. As he swung his feet out of the bed, he grabbed his pants he was going to wear and slipped them on. He has slept in his shirt and socks he'd been so tired. He worked his feet into his shoes, and hooked his leg over the bannister to slide down to the kitchen.

When he arrived at the bottom of the stairs, his mother grabbed him and hugged him.

"Oh, Taras, no one else slides down the bannister but you! I've missed you!"

He hugged her back and smile as he remembered she used to tell him not to wear our his pants.

"I've really missed you, too, Mother."

He slid onto the bench by Vadeem. Brother's plate held a half-piece of toast. No verinikes? He pictured the tasty dumplings with cheese or meat and sauce.

"Did you make verinikes, Mother? Aunt can't make them like you and Grandmother."

"No, Taras, there are no verinikes. There haven't been in a long time. Do you want to explain why, Serveig?" She glanced at his father.

"Son, we are very short in food. There is a famine in the Ukraine." His father's voice sounded sorrowful and distant.

"But the silos are full, Father. I saw them on the way, walking home. In fact, the grain is spilling over the top!"

"You are right, son; but it's no longer our grain; it's *theirs*."

"Their's? But, didn't we grow it, I mean you and Grandfather and Vadeem and the rest of the men in the village? So, it belongs to us!"

"That doesn't matter to them, the Kremlin. Stalin wants the grain for Russia to eat and tosell for export to other countries."

"That makes no sense; that's robbery! They can't take it; its ours!" Taras couldn't believe it!

"You're right, my son, exactly right, but now we have no control over it. They do."

That's what's meant by the occupation. They have the control. They have the guns!"

"Serveig, you didn't have to go that far!" His mother was frowning now, shaking her head.

"But it's the truth, Mother, it's the truth! If they didn't have the guns, we wouldn't stand for it!" This was the first time Vadeem had spoken." He might as well know the whole truth; he's growing up now."

Vadeem had never said that about him before. And Taras could see that he meant it.

"Oh, Taras, this is why we almost wanted for you to stay at Uncle's where you could eat, where you would be safe!" His mother was now pacing the floor.

"It is a dark day when you can't feed your children's hungry stomachs."

Grandmother, sitting beside him, hugged Taras with one arm.

"There's got to be a way!" Taras heard a question in his grandfather's low voice.

A loud knock interrupted the family's talk. Taras saw his brother take one bite of his toast and chew slowly, deliberately.

"Hurry up, we know you're in there! Don't waste our time!" Men's voices at the front door.

Father got up from his chair at the head of the table, pulled his body up straight, and walked to the front door and opened it.

Once again, Taras saw the black uniforms, black boots, heard their strident voices, and watched them push their way into the house past his father.

"Still at breakfast? If you had signed up for collective farming, you'd be having a much better breakfast at the farm; they have zatirka and tomatoes and potatoes."

The soldier sneered.

"Get ready and come up to the village square in two hours. You still have the opportunity to sign up for collective farming! You could be eating a lot more than one piece of toast for breakfast!" The soldiers took quick look around the kitchen and then laughed as they stomped out.

His father ground his teeth.

Taras took a small bite of his toast. He ate it slowly, like Vadeem.

An hour later, he walked with his father and grandmother to the village. Taras asked why they hadn't taken Victor and their cart.

"Because if they saw our fine, sleek, black stallion, they'd want him for their own!"

Grandfather answered.

"Yes," Taras agreed, "to match their fine leather boots! They'll never get out horse!"

Taras watched silently as they passed silos filled to their brim with grain. Hardly anyone was in their yards or gardens. The people they did see at their gates were leaving to go the same meeting and just nodded to them.

"Have you decided what we should do?" Grandfather turned his face toward Father.

"I despise to do it, but I don't have any choice! No choice! Isn't that something to say in our free Ukraine? We have to eat! That's the only reason I'll sign! My heart says

"No! No! No!" Father shook his head.

Grandfather nodded.

"If it weren't for the children and women, I'd rather starve first." Grandfather clenched his hands.

"And they took all our tools. What can we do without them? That's no small thing! They did it to force us to sign." Father shook his fist in the air.

In thirty more minutes, they reached the square. There were no more than fifty people there. A bullish-looking, short, swarthy man was talking to some of the people he recognized as the village's ruling council members. Taras remembered the last time he stood in the square. Everyone had been singing and dancing, celebrating a class graduating at the school. He looked around now and saw hungry, desperate faces and few women and no children.

The short bearded man stepped forward.

Chapter 4. Unity and Progress?

"I am Nicholas Nikiforov, district officer GP, in charge of this meeting. I represent our esteemed premier of the Soviet Republic, Josef Stalin. He asked me to extend congratulations to those of you who have already voluntarily signed up for collective farming. This is a big step forward for the unity and progress of our country."

Whose progress and whose country? Russia? Thought Taras. Certainly not the Ukraine. There was murmuring around him.

"Quiet! You want to hear everything I say. It is important! If you miss something, you won't know what to do."

They must think we are idiots, Taras thought.

"How many here are ready to sign? Just look at this list I brought of all the people who have signed up in other farming villages." Nikiforov waved a thick set of papers in the air.

"It's not fair to sign over the farm that's been in our family for two hundred years under the czars, that we've worked, so they can build their huge collective farms." A man behind Taras spoke up.

Nikiforov shouted, "All you who own 17-24 hectares are kurkels who must sign.

Or if you own three cows and several sheep and chickens, you must sign."

A dissenting voice declared he'd give away his cow to a neighbor who didn't have one first.

Nikiforov's face turned dark red.

He pointed to both men who'd spoken.

"You two come straight forward and start a line here in front of me." Since he brandished his pistol to make his point, the men hurried forward.

Nikiforov pulled a list from his pocket.

"I'm going to call eight names. If I call your name, step up with these men."

When the line was formed, Nikiforov summoned another officer.

"Board these men on a train for the north. They'll be working in the mines and lumbering. They won't need to pack anything. Everything they need will be there!"

There were many gasps in the crowd as they watched the men led away.

Taras heard no more mumbling. Everyone knew that the north meant Siberian work camps. No one wanted to go there.

"This meeting is now over. I'll be back in a week to sign up more of you. Think!

You might like no consider that you'd rather work on a collective farm here than be sent to Siberia."

Nikiforov walked briskly away to the railway station, not once looking back.

Grandfather nudged Father. "Did he make you so angry you wouldn't sign?"

"He made me furious. It's no wonder there's no much hatred." Father answered.

"We'll have to start eating the beets instead of selling them," Grandfather suggested. He steered Taras between them as they left the square and headed back home.

Moments later they passed a local general store. There was a long line.

"Actually, most of us need shoes. How about the women? Should we look while we're here?" Taras pointed at the store. He wanted the worry to be gone from their faces.

"Yes, all right," his father answered. He seemed distracted. They got in line.

"Were you at the meeting, Serveig?" Petras, a man in front of his father, turned to speak to them.

"We were there." Father answered and Grandfather nodded.

"I didn't sign, did you?" the man asked.

"No, I didn't. I don't know how we'll avoid it next time, though. We're lucky we weren't put on the train."

Taras reached for his father's elbow and held it. He didn't care who saw.

"Have you been in the shore since the soldiers came?" Petras asked.

"No, usually my wife does this while we're in the field, but we had to come to the meeting."

"The last time I worked in my field, the boundaries looked different." Petras sounded confused. "They wouldn't let us take anything home. Said Stalin's huge qoutas had to be met first. By the way, Father Dimitri has called a meeting of the men tonight at the swamp. Come as soon as the sun sets. Don't forget. And pass the word to your neighbors."

"All right, we will." Father promised.

"If we can't meet taxes, they can send us to prison for ten years or hard labor."

Grandfather spoke now.

"Yes, I heard that, too. They have raised them." Petras was interrupted by a soldier stepping into the street toward them.

"What are you looking to buy, today? He pointed at Father.

"Shoes, and some bread, meal, fat, and potatoes, that's all." Father made the list short.

"None of those are available. Only if you are working on the collective farm." The soldier was abrupt, Taras thought. And what did he mean, they couldn't buy?

"Come on, Taras, our shopping is over before it began." His father's voice was angry again. He took Taras's arm as they walked away from the store toward home.

Grandfather was shaking his head in disbelief.

"Now, by what's happened this morning, you understand occupation by the Russian, don't you Taras? His grandfather asked.

Taras nodded. He rolled his shirtsleeves down. He was getting chilly.

They heard someone running after them and turned to look back. It was Petras.

"My friends, I just was told that the only other way you can get something from the store is if you barter for what you want by having what they want. Say, you bring some silver if you have any or an heirloom."

"Is that what you did, Petras?" father asked.

"No, I don't have anything they want." Petras confessed.

"That's dishonest, isn't it?" Taras asked.

"Yes, growled his father, "because I'm sure they will sell anything we barter them for much more somewhere else.

All the men nodded in agreement.

Father spoke as they started home again. "I really hate to go home empty-handed."

"At least we are going home; think about that." Grandfather answered.

Taras thought of the full silos.

"We have to find a way to steal back some of "our" grain," he said.

"yes, but the silos are guarded. There is no safe way to do it," his father said.

"We are past the safe times; the boy is right, we have to eat." Grandfather's voice had a steel edge to it. Taras thought of the knife he used to whittle wood.

Chapter 5. GONE

Vadeem met them at the door when they came home.

"Come in; I know you're tired from walking, but there's bad news.."

"Wait until we get some tea, boy, all we've learned this morning has been bad news." Father wiped his feet on the doorstep and all three entered the house.

"Vadeem, he's right; the man un charge of the meeting was a tyrant." Taras stood Right in his brother's path.

"What a big word, little brother. Did you learn it this year?" Vadeem ruffled Tara's hair.

"I told you I wasn't little anymore, Vadeem!" Taras put his hand on his hips.

"I'm sorry, I forgot; tell me about this "tyrant.""

"He put ten men on a train to Siberia just because they wouldn't sign up for collective farming. I saw it. He didn't let them go home to pack or say goodbye to their Families. It was awful."

"You boys get to see everything! Why don't I ever get to go to important things?"

Luda looked like a thunderstorm beginning.

"Luda, I'm so glad you weren't there! It was unsafe. I wanted to hide." Taras hadn't meant to say that. He didn't want to sound afraid.

"Is what Taras said true, Serveig?" Mother came in bringing shirts she'd washed And hung on the attic line to dry. She went to the woodstove in the adjoining kitchen and lit a match for the teapot.

Taras looked up at the shawls draped around the religious pictures in the living Room. They look like arms reaching out to comfort us, he thought.

"I'm afraid so. Nikifrov is an evil man, for sure. He makes you know Stalin doesn't care what happens to the Ukraine. Starving us and deporting us if we don't sign."

"how are we going to eat, Ivan?" Grandmother looked at Grandfather.

"I don't know. We have to talk about that now. Make a plan to dry to get grain.

We've been selling beets to get money to buy from the store. Now you've found the money does us no good. We can't buy from the store unless we sign our land away to the Collective farm. And now the beets are about gone.

"Can't buy from the store?" Mother was incredulous.

"Yes, that's a new tactic, too." Father lowered his body into his chair.

"They're trying to kill us?" she asked.

"One way or the other. They seem to be, At least us kurkels."

"Speaking of that, I need to tell you what I saw today, or didn't see," Vadeem interrupted.

"Go ahead." Father looked at him.

"I stayed home and looked out for the women like you asked. I did leave for a few minutes to ride Viktor down to Stephan's farm. You know Stephan, right? He's Alex's father."

"Sure."

"Well, I found the strangest thing. It looked like their house had been ransacked.

There was also no one there, and the animals were missing, all of them."

"Oh no, Alex…" Taras covered mouth.

"You're right," Father agreed. "This is probably bad news. Was their food and clothing there?"

"No, all gone."

"Who would know about them that we could ask, Father?" Taras's voice wavered.

"How about Dimitri? He would tell us if he knows." Luda broke in.

"Good idea, Luda! He could probably tell us a lot of things." Taras remembered his sister had not been happy to have been left at home. "We could go this afternoon if we hurry."

"She can't go anywhere with you until I cut her hair!" Mother wanted.

"Cut my hair? Oh, no. I have something to say about that!" Luda jumped up from her chair, her hands on her hips.

"Luda, calm down. The last thing I want to do is cut your pretty black curls. There is no other way, though, I have no choice. Didn't you hear the soldiers commenting about your hair?"

"When was that?" Father frowned darkly.

"When they came through and took our tools. They said she was pretty and Vadeem was strong."

"Oh, me." Father shook his head. His eyes were blacker than usual.

"Well, I had an idea. If I cut her hair, and dress her in brother's clothes, then she'll look like a boy. Won't that be better?"

"Better?" Luda fumed under her breath. She started pacing around the room.

"Oh, yes, that would be better!" Taras teased her. He followed her, tapping her on the back to emphasize this point.

"You have to act like a boy, too. Luda; practice that, too, I can show you!"

"Mother, make him stop. He's awful." Luda burst into tears.

"Taras, you stop. You should know this isn't easy for her. What if I had to shave your head? How would you feel?"

Vadeem had put his arm around Luda. "It's all right, Luda. Please don't cry. You could never be ugly, even if Mother does cut your hair. And as a boy you could go places that girls could never go."

"I'm sorry, Luda, I didn't mean to hurt your feelings. Vadeem's right; it might be like an adventure, your going in disguise."

Luda stopped crying and looked at him. "An adventure?"

"Yes, we could say you are our cousin visiting from Kharkim. We could call you Yuri."

"That's actually a good idea, Taras." His father put his arm around Taras. He turned to look at Luda.

"No soldier is going is going to kidnap my girl because he thinks she's pretty and will make a nice girlfriend!"

"I don't even like boys!" Luda snapped. "So that won't happen!"

"They wouldn't stop and ask you. They'd just take you," Vadeem raised one eyebrow at his sister.

Chapter 6. The Secret

Luda had no answer for that. She reached for her mother's hand.

"May I start, then? Maria pulled the scissors from the drawer. She pulled a straight chair up for Luda to sit in and removed the multicolored rug from under her so it wouldn't catch the falling hair.

"It'll grow back out sometime, Luda." Her grandmother stepped forward to hug her. "Sometime when it's safer."

"The Russians bully us and worse; maybe we can outsmart them," Taras added.

"Can we have a sandwich first, Maria? We promise not to ask what kind of meat it is." Her husband was rubbing his stomach. "We also have to go a meeting at sundown with Dimitri. Petras told us this morning."

She nodded and went to the cupboard.

Taras wasn't about to ask what was in the sandwich. He just ate like everyone else and was glad for it. If Vadeem felt what they were eating was safe, he trusted him.

Vadeem pulled his knapsack and uniform from the closet when they had finished their sandwiches.

"I have a surprise. I found them when I left the Sokorov farm."

Taras watched with interest as his brother emptied cherries into an empty bowl.

"These are some the Russians missed, maybe while they were looting the house,"

Vadeem said as he passed the bowl to his grandmother. "They were on the trees lining the roadside going away from their farm."

"How wonderful," Mother said. "It was unselfish of you to save all these, Vadeem. Things have been hard, and we all are going to have to get used to sharing what we can find to eat." His mother rolled each cherry between her fingers, as if to prove it was real before she ate one. "One each; the rest are supper."

"They are wonderful, son. Thank you," said his father. "You were riding Viktor, weren't you? He's always been our steadiest horse. He held still while you pulled the cherries from the trees, right?"

That was a nice picture, thought Taras. Then he remembered that it was time to feed him.

"I'm going out to the barn. It's time to feed Viktor and the other animals."

I'll be out there in a few minutes," his father said, "I want to show you something."

It was a while before his father came out, but Taras didn't mind spending time with Viktor. He mounted the stallion and stroked his wonderful, sleek neck. Taras could tell Viktor was glad to have him back home. The horse threw his head back and forward smartly and neighed loudly. Taras leaned down to hug his neck.

"I missed you so much, Viktor. In the whole city of Kharkim they don't have a horse as handsome and smart as you." He slid down from the horse's back and faced him.

Viktor sniffed Taras' hand and pocket.

"I'm sorry, Buddy, there aren't any snacks for you. In fact, I'm wondering how we are going to feed you at all.

"I'm about to show you," Father answered as he entered the barn. He closed the door behind him.

"This is a secret. Make sure you don't tell anyone about this. Don't open it. Don't even look at it, if anyone at all is at the farm, not even our closest friends."

He stood in front of Viktor's stall and shoved aside the old hay from the floor.

Taras soon saw a door in the floor beneath them. It took all of Father's strength to lift it. Taras grabbed the other side without being asked. Underneath them he was amazed to see a cellar room, one that held beets? Could it hold people?

"We've been feeding us and the animals beets since the grain got scarce."

"Beets, I never heard of feeding animals those."

"Think about it. The iron they contain."

"You're right."

"it's one of the ways we've stayed alive, but they're almost gone."

Taras thanked God for the cow and goats, too. Milk.

"I've thought of a way I can help, Father," said Taras.

"Mother is cutting Luda's hair. She'll dress like a boy. She and I could go to the silo when it gets dark tonight and take back some of "our" grain. We're smaller and wouldn't be noticed like you adults would."

"That's brave but not safe enough, son. I know you're brave, but I'm afraid I'd lose you," Father said. "I'm your father and I say it's too dangerous!"

"Oh, I know, I was with you today at the meeting. But I'd make sure we were very careful. Luda and I could do it. I'd tell her it's like a play, except this time it's real."

"We could start tonight. We don't go to bed until after nine, anyway."

"You've become braver, my grandson."

Taras turned. He hadn't known Grandfather was behind them. Then he shrugged.

"We need grain, right? There aren't a lot of choices. It's a matter of life and Death." After he said it, the truth of it made him feel cold.

"If Vadeem ever went, he'd be noticed because he's tall and blond."

"Well, grandson. We heard someone say that strong young men and women might be taken to Russia to work in the factories they're building. You and Luda are the best candidates to go to the silos at night. You're much smaller that Vadeem. If they saw him, they might take him on the spot."

"I'll go tell Luda the adventure starts tonight, and that she has to be quite like a mouse. You know how we like to make up plays. She'll like this idea. After all, mice steal food and get away with it most times.

Taras was amazed at the transformation in Luda when they walked in the house.

He described what they were going to do later that night. She was dressed in some of Taras' clothes and looked for all the world like a boy, like a cousin named Yuri. Mother's eyes were red as if she'd been crying. But Luda was in the role already. She was practicing swaggering like a boy, shoving her hands in the pants pockets. She had on a cap with a bill that covered her bangs and she strode toward Taras and delivered a punch to his shoulder.

"Ouch," he complained, rubbing his arm. "That hurt!"

"Well, I suppose I'm ready," she said, and grinned at him,

Well, I got that adventure I was looking for, he thought. Just more than I wished for. Suddenly he realized the responsibility he was carrying tonight. He wasn't the only one going. His sister would be with him, too. He stood looking at her and thought she looked taller. She was. She was wearing old boots of his that were too small for him.

"Arm wrestle?" she asked.

"Later, maybe. We have to go to Dimitri's meeting now. Remember when we leave tonight, all has to be quiet. We can't yell out. We can't make any noise once we leave this house."

"I know."

"When we get back, it will be dark. Then, we'll leave."

"Mother, we're leaving when they return. Taras and I have to bring grain home."

Luda put her arm around her mother's shoulders.

Mother looked sadly at Luda. "I know," she said and looked out the window.

Taras knew his mother wished with all her heart it was not going to happen. Then he looked at Luda. His sister looked older then than she ever had. Much more than ten.

Chapter 7. Swamp Meeting

Dokia, the brown farm horse trotted eagerly as she pulled their cart to the swamp meeting. The little mare seemed glad to get out of the barn. Taras wished that Vadeem had come, but his father thought one of them should stay home with the women.

Why had the priest called a meeting at the swamp and asked just the men to come? He knew Dimitri must be worried about the village since the soldiers had come and were taking the grain. He was really worried. How were they going to eat? Did Dimitri know something new or have a plan? Taras had no idea, but he knew everyone would be happy to see Dimitri. One reason the people respected him was that he talked to them like his family. He didn't put himself above them.

Dimitri arrived on time with Petras and Volodya, a former teacher in Poldosk. He picked a higher slope to stand on, a bank of the reedy marsh so that he could see the crowd. Some black storks flying over the lake in the distance reminded Taras of the black uniforms in the village.

"Friends, you wonder, I am sure, why I called this meeting tonight. Tell the women I did not want to leave them out, but I knew the little ones would have to go to bed. When you get home, inform them of what we talk about here. Let them know I respect their thinking, and to share any ideas they have with you or me. Remember, Christ treated the women of his day with respect."

"Taras knew that some of the men differed with the priest on this subject. He was proud that his father and grandfather looked on his mother and grandmother as equals.

"Some of you have been saying that this time is no worse than 1897, or 1902. But since the Russians have been here, there is no question that we have been dealing with the worst of times in the Ukraine. Now our grain has been stockpiled for Russia's use, and we are in a critical state."

"We don't have enough to eat. They are stealing our grain," one man spoke up.

"Father, there are people already starving who were not healthy to begin with."

"That is exactly right and the reason I called this meeting. Have you found any Thing that helps you now, such as other things you can eat?"

"Beets, but they are scarce. We have given beet mash to the horse, too."

"Mushrooms, but some are poisonous."

"We have been giving the baby the milk."

"Yes, exactly."

"Linden leaves, pounded so they can be made into little cakes like corn cakes."

We hadn't heard of that before."

"We didn't ever fish before. We do now."

"There are fewer fish."

"Do you think of other things? I think of one. Treat your animal well. They are doing without food, too. What works for you may work for your neighbor if you tell him.

We can help each other. To survive, we will need to share our best information with our neighbor…what we find to eat in place of things we know to eat, when we rest, how we rest. We know when we feed our bodies less, we have to rest more. And if we have more, we can share some with a neighbor who has less or none.

There was mumbling among the men around Taras. He heard one say he didn't have anything to share.

"Do you remember that our Lord said that if we shared with others he would consider that we had shared with him? So need I ask if you your neighbor has a child and needs milk an you have a goat, if you would find it hard to share with that child?"

"By the way, if soldiers find their way to our meeting, we will begin singing a song as if that is the reason we're congregating. Praise or thanksgiving songs. We know a lot of those."

One man grumbled, "Thanks for what, for soldiers with guns?"

"For every new morning we are able to get up and see our families' eyes," Dimitri answered without pausing.

"How often we'll be able to have these meetings, I don't know, but the church has always been good at helping us find strength for our lives, especially in desperate times. I am proud to be your minister and friend. Call on me anytime. They may not let us meet in our church building, but they can't change my love for you, or yours for your neighbor.

Also, I'm sure all of you know by now; they have turned our church into a club.

They sent our bells to Russia to be used for industrial purposes. We cannot meet in our own church building."

Father Dimitri paused for the loud murmuring to die down.

"Remember, as these are hard times, we may be forced to do things we normally wouldn't. In defense of ourselves or our neighbors. We may need to be rescuers. We may need to be food finders or takers. Ask for God's strength and wisdom. He will provide it."

"Remember Joshua and Gideon; remember Samson. They thought they weren't important enough or strong enough to serve God or protect against the enemy. They were, with God's help."

"What we need are weapons, Father Dimitri. How can we defend ourselves?"

The priest studied the man for a moment and the said, "How did David slay Goliath? By not fearing to do what he could do. My friends we need to share not only our food, but our best ideas and ways of doing things. We need to practice what we're good at, like David did, so that when our special times come, we are ready."

"I have thought of one plan, a way I might can help as your priest. The soldiers give me leftovers from their table each night at six. One of them is sympathetic with our plight. He brings more. Any food I can share with you, I will. You have in your homes a list of church members. Starting tomorrow night, the first one on the list should come to my shed back of the church, around six-thirty. I will share with that person, and he will tell the next person who is to come the following night. If it should become dangerous to come there, we'll decide another place for us to meet. Maybe we will alternate places to prevent suspicion. You see, I don't expect you to do anything I am not willing to do myself."

"It's been good to be with you. I may no longer be allowed to wear clerical clothes, and we can't have church on Sunday, but I still feel like your priest. Now God go with you. Be aware; pray for each other; take care of each other."

It had grown very quiet, Taras thought, as people left to go home. It had been a different kind of church meeting. A secret church. He shivered when he remembered the early Church had had to meet in the catacombs. The swamp wasn't so bad. There were no tombs here. One just had to watch out for occasional snakes.

Chapter 8. Scavenging Grain

After Father, Grandfather, and Taras returned from the swamp meeting. Taras and Luda got ready to go. The moon hung low over the horizon, but Taras hoped for a cloud cover to come along. If it were too clear a night, the guards might be able to spot them if they heard a noise. On the other hand, though, a moon could help them. They'd be better able to see what they were up against. As they left the house, his father told them to tie Viktor in the little stream's gulley before they reached the silo. That way the soldiers wouldn't hear him if he whinnied.

Taras and Luda both wore jackets to have somewhere to hide grain they might find. Grandmother had cut and sewn the tops of the lining inside for that purpose. His mother hugged them hard to her and then left the room. She wasn't able to speak. Father grabbed them before they opened the door to leave.

"God go with you my children. Be very careful. If there was any other way..."

"We know, Father. We will."

Outside the barn, Taras helped Luda up onto Viktor's back and then swung himself up behind her. Viktor neighed impatiently. He seemed to be excited that the children were taking him out for a late night ride.

"It's just as well you don't know where we're going, Viktor. You might try to break into the fence to get some grain for yourself!"

"Don't even say the word. 'grain'; Taras; I think he knows it." Luda grabbed the reins to hold on tight.

"Good thinking, Luda, you've gotten smarter while I was gone."

Taras noticed she sat straighter at the compliment. He should remember to encourage her more. It was important that she feel confident for these strikes on the silo.

"You know we're actually going to have to trade seats so I can see where we're going. You've gotten taller this year."

"All right," Luda said and slid to the ground.

When Taras had exchanged places with Luda, he took the reins.

"Hold on to my waist; remember we can't make any noise once we get near the field. You will see or hear some things you don't like. You won't be able to say anything or do anything, though. We can't fail at getting grain. The family is depending on us."

"I know, Taras; I'll be quiet. You show me what I should do; I'll do it."

Luda had never spoken to him that way before.

One of the village silos was located about five miles away from the houses at the side of the fields where Father and Grandfather had worked the land for many years.

Now he realized that their smaller fields had become part of the sozholk now, the bigger collectivized farm. Whether they wanted it or not, it was about to happen. He remembered what Petras had said at the store about not being able to see the boundaries.

There had been no fences. A line of birch trees had been the marking for where their land ended. Petras had said the Russians didn't care about their village boundaries or field boundaries so they were disappearing. They were stealing their grain and their land.

Taras held Viktor back to a gentle trot. Viktor pulled at the reins. He clearly wanted to run faster. Normally Taras would have let him go, but now he was wondering if they could have been quieter and hidden better without Viktor. Well, tonight they'd find out if this way worked. His stomach was full of butterflies. He slowed down a little to talk to Luda. She was probably nervous, too. He wished his big brother could have come; he'd have felt safer.

Taras, why didn't we bring a scoop for the grain?"

"That might have helped: we forgot, Luda. We don't even know if we'll be able to get at any grain. They may have it fenced in so well that it won't spill under the fence, or the wall of the silo. I don't even know how silo looks anymore. It used to be wooden and two-story like a house. Up off the ground some. They may build them out of blocks, now, for all I know. We'll just have to see the situation when we get there."

"What Father said was it was guarded. We know that, right?"

"Absolutely, you can count on that."

Luda was shaking. He was sorry his sister had to go through this. It was just one more fact that made him angry. He felt her lay her head against his back.

He tried to think what their mother would have told her.

"It's all right, Luda; it's going to be all right. You'll see. Take deep breaths; it might make you feel better."

Taras was not sure anything was ever going to be all right again, but he did not want Luda to know his doubts.

"I'm not Luda anymore, Taras. Will I ever be Luda again?" Her voice was sad.

"You're right; was it Bony or Skinny, you were supposed to be?"

"Taras, you silly boy, it's Yuri; don't you remember?' Luda giggled. She pulled his ear.

What he didn't say was that he could tell they'd all lost weight. He wondered how much

"Oh, 'Yuri', that's right; see, it's good you have a memory."

Suddenly he realized Viktor was running faster. He had loosened his hold on the reins while they were talking. He pulled Viktor up closer. The horse slowed back to trot.

"Taras, why is it so dark and quiet? I haven't seen any lights in the houses we've passed. It's still early. Won't people wonder why we have on jackets? It's not cold."

"It's night, Luda; probably no one will think of that." He hoped. His sister was asking some good questions. "they won't see us well enough to notice."

Suddenly in the distance he saw what looked a fire. Probably for the guards at the silo, he thought. He pulled the reins up tight to stop Viktor.

"We'll have to tie Viktor up here and go the rest of the way on foot, Yuri," he told his sister. He slid down and helped his sister down off the horse's sweating back.

"I'm glad I can run fast, Taras, if I have to."

"That's right, Yuri, you can." It was hard to think of his sister as a boy.

Viktor wanted to follow them. Taras gave him a beet from his pocket to munch on, and he settled down, chewing contentedly.

"Yuri, hold my hand; we'll walk close together, until I see how things are laid out."

Luda took his hand. They crept closer to the fire and the silo. As they neared the site, they saw four soldiers sitting around a fire.

Chapter 9. The Lookout

The silo was two-story wood as Taras had remembered. There was enough space underneath it. It looked like there was enough space to crawl under it out of sight if they needed to.

It appeared there was some kind of canvas off the front side where the men were sitting. That was good. If they went to the back, they wouldn't be seen as easily. They had crawled the last few yards so they would look more like dogs or animals that people if they were spotted. When they were close to the back, they heard voices Taras recognized.

"Don't be piggish with the bottle, Fritz, pass it along." Taras remembered Fritz from the train station. He'd been too evil to forget.

"Why don't you just come and make me give it to you, Vasty? We have nothing to do out here anyway; we should have brought cards from the club.

"I don't know why they sent us to this god-forsaken place," Vasyl complained.

"I can't wait to get back to Moscow. The city. This place is beginning to get on my nerves. I'm going to ask if I can't go back and guard a factory, the palace, or something."

"Fritz," I said. "Pass the bottle."

"And I said, come and get it. Two to one, you aren't strong enough, sissy!" Fritz stood, took a swig from the bottle, and waved it in Vasyl's face.

"You hog, you'll see!" Vasyl jumped up and lunged at Fritz, knocking him to the ground. He got one lick at Fritz' jaw, but then the younger man rolled out of reach.

The soldier on the other side of Fritz grabbed his arm and wrstled the bottle from it. he took a long draw from the bottle and passed it to Vasyl.

"What bet was that you made, Fritz, two to one? You owe me." Vasyl smirked

"You had to have help to get the vodka; I'm not paying you anything. You better sleep with both eyes open tonight, Vasyl."

"We don't trust you, Fritz. We always sleep with our eyes open."

Taras and Luda had lain very still and watched the men from under the silo. Taras had relished seeing Fritz bested by the other soldiers. In a few minutes, the bottle was empty. The soldiers grabbed their knapsacks to use for pillows and settled down.

"All right, Boris, you're on watch 'til morning. Keep a careful eye." Fritz directed.

"Always," was Boris' answer.

Thank God, beathed Taras. Boris, the older, kind soldier from the train station.

The voice came from a space to the left of Taras. Up high in the tree. From a stand. Was it a watchstand? Had Boris seen them? Taras had to trust his instincts; he couldn't call out.

Luda pulled at his sleeve. She pointed to the corner. She had spotted a mound of grain that had leaked through a hole in the floor of the silo. It probably wasn't visible from the outside. They crawled over to it and noiselessly started filling their jacket linings with the grain. Twice in the process, Taras stopped them to listen for noise.

When the two had finished collecting the mound of grain, Taras reached up to the opening and felt for more. He couldn't make the grain come down, he didn't think, without noise.

"Let's go," he whispered to Luda. "My jacket's full; is your?" She took his hand to feel her face and nodded her head up and down. He crept out from under the silo and quietly stood up. Luda followed suit, copying everything that he did. He had a feeling that Boris might have seen them come and now go. He looked up the tree trunk, but he couldn't see anything or anybody. There was no sound. Very stealthily and quietly, Taras moved across the road. Luda silently followed him.

When they got to the trees on the other side of the road, they were able to keep skulking down the road under cover of them. Viktor must have smelled the grain as they reached him. He nuzzled Taras' coat and whinnied.

"Shhh, boy, shhh." The horse obeyed. Taras untied the rope and looked back at the camp they just left. There was no movement or noise. Maybe the men had drunk enough to be fast asleep by now, he hoped. He pulled himself up on the horse's back, took the reins and reached down to give Luda a hand up. She pulled up and into the saddle and reached around his middle to hold on. He gave a little to Viktor, and they walked slowly at first, moving into a trot only when they were farther down the road When they drew closer home, they saw another fire on the horizon.

"Oh Taras, what in the world is that?" Luda's voice shook.

"I don't know..." he answered worriedly.

As the horse brought them closer by, they recognized the house. It was the home of a neighbor known to be an activist against the collectivization. Taras had a horrible feeling that fire was no accident. Luda held to him tightly as they slowed to a shop, then trotted the horse up as close to the roaring fire as was safe. The roof was collapsing.

The curtains were blazing in the windows. The fire made Viktor very nervous. He tried to bolt away. Taras held him as steadily as he could and called out as they circled the house.

"Spolinsky, Spolinsky, are you there? Anybody, are you there?" The only response they heard was the terrible crackling of the fire. There was no one, no one.

Chapter 10. Fires and Nightmares

Taras and Luda found no place to enter Spolinsky's house safely. Every entrance was a blazing inferno. There were no neighbors' houses close by to go to and ask for help. They raced Viktor home. At the gate they slid off Viktor's back, tied him to the fence post and half-fell up the porch steps in their hurry.

"Father, Grandfather, get up, get up!" shouted Taras. "There's a fire at Spolinsky's house!"

They burst in the front door together.

"Their house is falling in!" Luda called out, panting to catch her breath.

"A fire at Spolinsky's?" No one could believe it.

"We didn't see anyone with hoses or water," Taras gasped.

"We didn't see anybody at all! Where could they be?" Luda cried.

Father and Grandfather were out the door in seconds.

"How can we help them? It's so awful, awful! What if that happened to our house? Where are they? The house was falling in! Oh, Grandmother!" Luda buried her head in her grandmother's shoulder and sobbed. Grandmother held her in her arms until she grew quiet.

Remembering the grain, Taras and Luda took off their coats to remove it from their pockets. Mother and Grandmother were delighted and hurried to the kitchen to find containers for it. the women were amazed at what the children had.

Grandmother pulled two jars from the cabinet.

"I had no idea you'd even be able to get any. Those guards have really been thick everywhere. No one's had much luck, we've heard." As soon as the grain was in the jars, Vadeem put them in his knapsack.

"I'll take this amount to the swamp tonight to grind as soon as Father and Grandfather get back. Wonderful! We have really needed this... this grain." Vadeem's voice broke. His brother wiped his face on his shirtsleeve, but Taras suspected that Vadeem was worrying about what would happen once they'd eaten it all.

"Why are you grinding at the swamp, Vadeem?' Taras scratched his head.

"Because if we grind it at the big mill they would take at least 25 per cent of it for the taxes we owe and can't pay. That's because they've taken our grain that we made our living from!"

"Can't we keep a mill here at the house?"

"No, they take those, too, on their searches. They'd get suspicious that we had grain if they found a mill here.

An hour later the men came in the front door. They were sooty from the smoke nnd looking for the family

"We must pray for Spolinsky and his family," said Grandfather, shaking his head.

"We found no sign of any of them, and the...the house is destroyed." His grandfather's voice sounded like he was announcing a death.

"I think the person who started that fire took the animals," Father shook his fist.

"You think somebody set the fire on purpose, Father?" That idea scared Taras.

"I'm afraid there have been others, son."

"How awful; how could somebody burn another person's house down?"

Taras' question was to anyone, but no one said anything.

Finally, Mother said they should go to bed if there wasn't anything they could do.

"I really hate Vadeem is having to go to the swamp this late; he's tired. You're going to see Father Dimitri, tomorrow, right, Taras?" Mother asked

"I'm going, too!" Luda spoke up.

"That you are; I'm so proud of you and your brother." Mother hugged her daughter to her.

Thoughts of the terrible fire kept Taras from sleeping that night, and it haunted Luda's sleep, too. Taras heard her talking in her sleep through the wall between their bedrooms.

Taras' stomach actually hurt from hunger the next morning. He had never had that feeling before. His father had always made a good living. Vadeem had said, though, that there had been no flour to make bread from that day. There had been no supper. Maybe Vadeem and I should try fishing tomorrow, he thought.

When he checked his brother's bed in the room across from his, he noticed his brother was still in a deep sleep. Vadeem's eyes had dark circles under them from the late night at the swamp. Maybe from worry, too, like the other grownups, he thought.

Coming down the stairs he heard the adults talking. He paused on the steps.

"I could not rest the whole time Taras and Luda were gone last night." His mother's voice.

"No one could, my dear." That was his father.

"Do you remember the famine ten years ago?" Katrina, his grandmother said.

"Who could forget?" His grandfather said.

"That was before I was born." Luda said.

"Was it like this one? I'm too young to remember." Taras walked into the kitchen.

The sun had come though the lace curtains and made a lovely pattern on the opposite wall behind his sister, The red colors in the tapestry hanging on the same wall shone brightly. It had always been a cheerful room in which to eat, he thought.

"A drought caused that famine. No enemy occupied the Ukraine. We had no food then because of the drought. Now there is plenty of food, but guards keep it from us and send some to Russia to feed them and export some to make money for Stalin to industrialize Russia." His father spoke and dug his hands in his pant's back pockets.

"It was easier to deal with, an act of nature, not soldiers, thievery, and guns." His mother added and wiped her wet hands on her apron.

"Here's hot tea, everyone." His grandmother sat down the brightly-flowered red, brown, and gold cups and saucers. "When you come home, hopefully, bread."

"Here's to bread, tonight, maybe!" His father lifted his cup.

The others all lifted their cups as well.

"Bread, please, God," his grandmother prayed.

Chapter 11. Looking For Father Dimitri

The women hugged the children at the door.

"Take Viktor, in case you need to make a quick exit. Make him look ugly. Put dust on his coat. Otherwise, he'll draw too much attention."

They followed their mother's instructions.

"Taras, do you want me to ride in back, again?"

"Yes, that's good."

The children were soon on their way to the village and the church.

"Taras, do you feel like there's a hole in your stomach?" Luda sounded sad.

"Mine actually hurts," Taras answered. Do you think yours has shrunk?"

"I'm sure it has. I've lost weight. I had to draw these pants up tighter today since there was no supper. Maybe we'll at least have bread and borscht tonight. Please, God.!"

"It's hard to think of anything but food when you're so hungry. What did you do when you couldn't eat while I was gone?" Taras rubbed his belly to see if that would help.

"I tried to read, but it was hard to concentrate. I've dreamed of food, all my favorite things. It's really hard when you wake up from that dream and know there's nothing in the kitchen."

"I don't see Ivan and Ilsa's goat today. When I walked home that first day from the train station. He was trying to climb the fence to get to what was left in the yard garden."

"They may have eaten him by now, Taras; I hate to say it, but things have been that hard.

"Luda, I feel so guilty you have gone through this; I haven't been here." Taras shook his head.

"Sometimes, I get lightened from not eating; I feel like I'm going to faint."

Luda laid her head against his back.

"Maybe Dimitri will have something you can eat, Luda. He's a kind person."

Taras patted his sister's knee.

"A lot of the village people are kind, Taras; they just haven't had food to share."

Taras realized Luda was rubbing Viktor's side.

"I can tell where his ribs are; Taras, that makes me very sad."

"I know."

"There's the old candy store; it's closed today." Taras pointed to the right.

"It's closed all the time, pretty much, now. Nobody has money for candy."

"I don't want candy, anyway; I just want bread, don't you?"

"Yes."

The children rode along silently for a while. Taras realized for the first time it took energy to talk.

"People take more naps now, Taras; we're all tired, faster. It makes me understand for the first time how people could steal if they're hungry, or if their children are hungry."

They passed a café on the corner. The only people inside were soldiers.

"There's the church. I'll tie Viktor here to this tree in the shade. He doesn't look too handsome, does he?" Taras made a handprint in the dust on Viktor's back.

"No, don't help me down, Taras, remember, I'm Yuri."

Taras nodded. Yuri slid down carelessly, like a boy might. Taras tied Viktor.

They walked up to the front door of the church and knocked. The flag on the front was a Russian one.

A Russian soldier appeared at the front door.

"Yes, what is it?" He spoke gruffly and looked unhappy at the interruption.

"Speak up, you are keeping me from my game!" He was scowling now.

Behind the man Taras saw soldiers at a table playing cards. They were smoking cigarettes and drinking from brown bottles. Beer, probably.

"We are looking for Father Dimitri?" Taras spoke up.

"Yes, Do you know where he is?" Luda slouched the way a boy would.

"Out back, out back!" The soldier slammed the door in their faces.

In back they didn't see anyone so they stepped up to the door of the shed in the yard. Taras tried the door. It wasn't locked. He knocked.

A moment later Dimitri was in the doorway, looking both surprised and happy.

"Taras! Oh, how good it is to see you! Come in, your friend, too."

Inside, Luda noted, "This must be a good disguise. I am Luda, Father."

"Luda, heavens! I thought you were a boy. Your long curls, all gone!"

"I am a boy. Yuri is my name. I am Taras's cousin from Kharkim."

"Very clever, Yuri, you say? All right! Good idea, too. Who came up with that?"

"My mother," said Taras.

"Smart woman, very inventive."

"Father, what are you doing back here in the shed, wearing everyday clothes?"

"I am an everyday man, now Taras. Doing everyday things like polishing these boots for the soldiers, cleaning the barracks, cooking meals for them. The Russians don't think the church is important anymore. They think it is a threat to the State and to their "workers paradise." So, they have taken our bells away to use in their factories. They have made the church into a club for drinking and gambling. They were going to send me to Siberia to work until they had the idea I could wait on them here. They tried to get a woman to cook for them, but she almost succeeded in poisoning them. We haven't seen her since. They said I could stay out here in the shed as long as I understood I was their servant."

"Is that what the Lord meant when he said we were to be servants?" Luda looked puzzled.

"Not at all, my dear; this is the Russian variety; you remember the serfs? I van has told you about them, right?

"Yes, they were like slaves. The czars were cruel to them."

"Exactly. The Russian say they want all men to be equals, but apparently the Ukrainians are not as equal as Russians."

"What happened to your house, Dimitri?"

Dimitri looked down.

"They didn't like my leaving here to go home at all so they took my house to use for themselves. They gave me a cot for out here."

"How terrible, Father, we are so sorry. What will you do?"

Dimitri shrugged.

"You, my friends, don't deserve to be hungry, either. Speaking of that, there is a good thing about my being out here in the shed. Occasionally people come to me I can help."

"Sometimes I've smuggled food out of the church kitchen. Sometimes I've given directions to where someone is, or a place they need to reach. As you know, a lot of things have changed here.

"They control our village! Nothing to eat! They steal everything, our grain, our animals, houses."

"Taras, Luda, never let them steal your compassion or your sense of right and wrong, your faith. Promise me."

"We won't Father. We've missed you and church."

"You know, children, hard times sometimes cause you to have to do hard things."

"What do you mean exactly? Hard times like now? Luda seemed puzzled.

"For instance, wearing that disguise as a boy is not something you ever planned to do. It's taking a risk if the soldiers happened to find out, but it's a lot safer than being out by yourselves with you dressed as a normal girl.

"Mother did explain that to me."

"I'm always here, children. I'm glad we had this talk. Right now, I better get these boots polished. Oh, here's a letter to read when you are out of town, toward home. Don't open the envelope until then."

Taras thought the envelope felt more like it held a sandwich. That would be like Dimitri. He hid it in his inside jacket pocket.

Outside, the children had to shade their eyes from the bright sun. They trudged off to where they had tied Viktor to a tree. He was surely whinnying a lot. Maybe there was a burr in his mane. When they got ready to mount, Luda yelled out, to Taras.

"This isn't Viktor! This isn't Viktor!"

The horse was the same size as Viktor but BROWN. Where was Viktor?

Chapter 12. The Wrong Horse

Taras' eyes searched the square. He knew this tree was exactly the one to which he'd tied Viktor. It was far enough away from the church that soldiers wouldn't notice him, but someone had taken his horse. And left him this horse which seemed old and tired.

"What a terrible trick!" Luda spouted and stepped back from the horse.

"They're trying to see what they can get by with; well, I'll show them. There is Viktor tied over there behind that office. We'll just go get him!"

Luda scurried to follow Taras who was running to his horse.

Viktor nodded his head up and down when he saw them. Then he tried to twist out of the rope around his neck, to get to Taras.

"Steady, Viktor, I'll get you loose."

Taras grabbed the bridle at the of his horse's head.

"It's all right, Viktor; I've got you now. We're here."

"Hey, what do you think you're doing with my horse?" Taras and Luda turned to see a well-dressed Russian officer walking toward them from the church.

"He's not your horse; he's mine. My family's."

"Stand away; your horse is over across the yard, that brown one. I left him for you.

"Consider yourself fortunate. We usually just take what we want. This time I traded mine for yours. Our stables are full of such horses. We don't have room for this broken-down one. So, take him and leave."

"No, this is my horse; I don't want yours. Anybody can see he's old and worn out."

"Precisely why I need a new one, a fine black steed like this one to match my black boots and black uniform. All you need is the brown horse to pull your plow.

"Now, take your hand from the bridle."

Taras looked down to hide his anger. He wasn't letting go of his horse!

"No!" he yelled and held the rope fast, gritting his teeth. There was a sudden crack in the air. He jerked as the soldier's whip lashed his hand. Blood ran down his wrist.

"Do you or your friend there want to argue with my whip?" The soldier drew it back to crack it again. Taras backed in front of Luda.

"No, we'll do as you say! Taras spit out the words. He had to protect Luda.

He stood well away from Viktor, now, and pulled Luda close beside him.

"Now, my beauty, I expect you need a lesson in obedience, too. If you belong to me, you will obey me." He advanced toward Viktor and drew back the whip again.

It cracked across Viktor's back. The black horse rose up an clawed the air, lunging at his enemy. Before the soldier could jump back, Viktor's hooves struck his chest.

"Agh, aggh, Help! It's a demon horse!" The soldier, on the ground, now, tried to scuttle backward away from Viktor as the horse bared his teeth.

The soldier's cohorts came outside to watch the excitement. He screamed at Taras.

"Get that devil out of here; he tried to kill me. He's possessed! Control him!"

Taras jumped quickly to grab Viktor's reins. He yanked the rope loose.

The children swung up on his back. Taras let Viktor gallop before the officer changed his mind.

"Thank God he let us have Viktor back!" Luda held on so tight to him he could hardly breathe.

"Viktor won't ever forget him. He better keep his distance," Taras told her.

"Taras, he had a pistol; it's a wonder he didn't try to shoot us."

"He might have." Taras' eyes caught glimpse of another CLOSED sign. It was hanging on thew school's front door. What a lonely sight; no kids were playing in the schoolyard.

"Luda do you see that? The school is closed!"

"Father told us they sent the two teachers to work on the collective farm. Stalin said they needed people to work more than teach. Mother thought those were Communist drill songs they were teaching us."

"They probably can close it; like Vadeem says, they have the guns."

"Whoa, Viktor, whoa." He pulled the reins up.

Taras, why are you stopping?"

"Do you think they locked up the books, Luda?"

"I don't know. No one said."

In the late afternoon sun his mind went back in time to a skit that his class had done about several leaders who had encouraged "free Ukraine". He'd played Taras Shevchencho, the poet who had told the Ukrainians they had to get free from the czars.

The poet had preached that there was no change for individual growth of the people under the oppression of the czars.

"Taras, what are you thinking?" asked Luda.

"We are going to fight back."

"How?"

"With books, for one thing. We're going to take what textbooks we can carry home. They can't take our brains or keep us from learning."

They circled back of the schoolhouse. There the schoolyard also included a soccer field, play yard, and gym, all empty.

"I miss my friends," Luda cried. "I miss Miss Polansky, too."

"She taught you art. You paint well, but Mother could teach you more now."

"Remember Vadeem's music teacher who recognized his ear for music?"

"He hasn't played for us in a long time."

"Maybe when he eats tonight, he'll have the energy to do it."

"Break this window; no one can see you. I'm glad you thought of getting the books, Taras. It will help us."

Taras took off his boot to break the window. When he had climbed through the window opening to see if it were safe, he helped Luda through.

"Help me look in these boxes on the table. Maybe they're the books we would be studying this year, Luda."

She moved beside him and opened one.

"Here are the ones for your class, Taras." She handed him the next which he quickly put in the long inside pocket of his jacket.

He felt the envelope Dimitri had given him. He took it from his pocket and tore it open to find two pieces of bread and meat to share and a slice of cake. They divided it between them and ate it slowly.

"That tasted like heaven," Luda breathed. Taras agreed.

"We need to feel stronger; we're going to have to scavenge again tonight or tomorrow. Thank you, Dimitri; God protect you," Taras prayed quickly.

"This book is the one for the fourth grade, Luda." He handed a text to her. She slipped it into the inside pocket of her jacket.

"I didn't think I'd ever steal textbooks from the school, did you. Taras?"

Taras laughed a little.

"I used to leave them behind so I'd have an excuse not to do homework."

"We can always bring them back when school starts up again."

"Right." Taras surely hoped that was going to happen. Right now he couldn't believe it.

Suddenly his sister put her finger to her lips.

"What's that noise?"

Chapter 13. Brush Torches, Vadeem?

"It's horses, lots of them!"

They hurried to the front windows. A large group of soldiers raced by. Some were carrying brush torches. They weren't lit yet, but why they carrying them?

"Taras, where are they going?" Luda's face was white.

"I don't know. I think we should follow them."

"Let's get Viktor!"

Outside, the books safely in their jackets, the two mounted Viktor and struck out toward the galloping sounds of the horses.

They never got within sight of them, but somehow realized they were getting closer home, and the sound never went away. Finally as they approached the last bend in the road, they saw the front of their house. In the yard the soldiers all sat on their horses.

There were loud voices.

Father and Grandfather stood on the front steps.

It seemed the captain was talking, or whoever was in charge.

They pulled Viktor into the woods next to the house to listen.

"Ivan and Serveig, you never signed the form for collective farming!"

We came to encourage you to do that." They waved the torches.

Taras heard Luda gasp behind him.

"You needn't have brought torches to threaten us with. We slready decided to sign. You didn't call a meeting for that to happen." Father stood tall and unafraid. Taras had never been prouder of him. Grandfather stood like a giant beside him. Taras felt his heart swell.

"We always like to make a personal call on you, Serveig, see the family and such.

Where are they, by the way?" This man must be Fritz's relative, thought Taras. Equally evil. He handed Viktor a beet to eat, to keep him quiet. It sounded as if Luda were praying.

"Not feeling so well. Maria and Katrina are weak from eating enough. As are We. How is the collective farm plan going to work if the workers are so hungry and weak they can't be productive?"

"Not for you to worry about. Your food will increase immediately. When you go to the farm to work tomorrow, you can eat there. And we expect everyone to report by sunrise. Understood?"

"I think your meaning is very clear." Grandfather's face did not hide his feelings.

He was probably gripping the porch post iron-tight to keep his anger inside.

A soldier at the back of the group shouted something to the commander.

The commander laughed out loud.

"My comrade wants to know when we light the torches. I told him we weren't going to need them after all. He's disappointed."

There were more loud comments from the man. Others laughed.

"He was cursing in Russian. Do you want the translation?"

"It's not necessary." Father spoke in Ukrainian to Grandfather.

"What did he say, Ivan?" The commander wanted to keep control.

"I didn't hear it well." Ivan answered.

Taras thought he knew. His father had always said swearing was unnecessary.

Why were the Russians so good at it?

"Well, sorry we have to leave you now.; we must visit others on our list."

As the soldiers rode out, they turned to go inside, but then they saw a man leading his horse up to their yard. There was a figure lying across its back. He had long blonde curly hair, looked young but acted lifeless. All the family rushed forward.

"Oh dear God, it's Vadeem! Is he all right?" Mother had run out of the house.

"I think he is; he passed out from hunger when were milling the grain. I am Olifirenko. We have been milling together at the swamp. Here is the flour he ground."

The man pulled out the bag from the saddle and handed it to Mother.

"Don't feed him too much at a time. Do it gradually. Some have died from finding leftover grain in the fields and eating too much, too fast."

"Thank you; God bless you for bringing him home." Father picked up Vadeem in his arms. Ivan helped carry his legs.

"He's kind, young man, your son. I was glad to help him. He ground for me one night when I was weak.

Grandmother stepped forward and touched the man's arm.

"I thank you, too. In this awful time we need to help each other. Here are some beets for you and your family."

"Dyakuyu." (Thank you) "Vadeem seems somewhat bloated. A doctor in our village, Moishe Fishbank, has been saving some starving people by feeding them snails from the riverbank. He doesn't know why it works, but it decreases the bloating."

Taras promised himself he and Luda would go fishing the next morning. He touched his brother's forehead and smoothed his hair from his face after the men laid him on the couch in the front room.

"I had thought we would go fishing together, brother, but this time Luda and I Help you. Please get better." He noticed Luda had wiped her eyes when she bent to kiss her brother's cheek.

"Luda, maybe we can find the snails for him tomorrow." He smiled as he saw his sister shudder. Then she stood taller.

"Anything for Vadeem, Taras." She sat down on a chair nearby to watch him.

"I'm going to make pirogues with some of this flour. That's Vadeem's favorite."

Mother looked worried and her voice trailed off…

"All right, then I'll give him some of this borsch first, then." Grandmother was spooning it into a bowl. "It's bound to taste better than thar Linden leaf concoction we've had to eat.

Taras wondered where his grandfather and father had gone. He looked out the front window for them. Now anytime a member of the family was out of sight, he was going to worry. And going to work at the collective farm? How could that be a good thing? And how could they be sure that even doing that would save their lives?

Chapter 14. The Fishing Trip

Taras woke up thinking about his brother, hoping today Vadeem would be on his feet and back to his old self. Sliding into his clothes, he didn't stop to knock on Luda's door as usual. He bypassed the kitchen and turned into the living room. There he knelt down on the wood floor by the couch where his brother lay asleep. Vadeem's eyes were closed, but Taras could watch his chest rise and fall.

"Thank God," he whispered aloud, though the breaths seemed ragged and rough.

Then he stood up and wandered to the kitchen where his grandmother was making Linden leaf pancakes for breakfast.

"What can Luda and I do for Vadeem?" he asked her.

"You could go to the river fishing;" she answered, "the fish would give him strength." She slid the pirogues onto a plate and cut them into tiny pieces.

"You're saving the pirogues for Vadeem?" Taras looked longingly at them.

"Maybe the smell of his favorite dish will bring him around."

"God willing. You mother and I watched him during the night. He opened his eyes and sipped a little borsch but didn't talk because he's so weak. We fed him slowly and gave him small bites of dumpling at a time so he wouldn't choke."

"Luda and I will try to catch some fish today."

"Be careful. Father and Grandfather went to the collective farm early."

"We will."

Taras shook his head. He concentrated on sending the linden cakes to his stomach, not on how they tasted. He had hoped for pirogues this morning, but he certainly didn't mind if his brother had them instead.

Luda interrupted his serious mood and pushed his elbow he'd been leaning on, off the table. "How am I doing as a boy?" She asked.

"Too well," he said, kneeing her sideways under the table.

"I am so tired. A nap…"

"No nap yet."

"All right, Taras."

They dragged their feet to the barn to get Viktor. He ate the beet mash quickly;

Luda looked puzzled.

"Taras, why do horses never get tired of the same grain or mash, day after day?"

"They have never had all the different foods we have, Luda. You could list on one hand all the foods Viktor has had."

"And I couldn't list on both hands and feet all the foods we've eaten. Do you think Viktor likes beets as well as apples now, Taras?"

"Shh. Don't even say that word! I'm sure he remembers how good they are!"

"I'm sorry, Viktor," Luda said and laid her cheek on the horse's neck.

As they rode across the steppe to the river, Taras heard Luda sighing.

"Is it Vadeem?"

"Yes, I'm really worried about him."

"He's going to be all right, Luda. He's eating."

"But he's not talking."

"He will; just give him time."

"Taras, the other day I saw him put his own dinner on our plates."

"Really?"

"Yes, and I heard Mother say to Father, 'Feed the children first.'"

"You listen well, Yuri."

"He's got to be all right. He's my brother!"

She grabbed Taras's shoulder tightly and held on to him. Her head lay against his back. Her voice was muffled.

Viktor pulled on the reins. Taras loosened his hold on them and let Viktor run.

"He knows we're headed to the river," Luda guessed.

At the river the children watched the horse drink. Then they tied him to one of the birch trees on the bank and threw in their lines.

"Is the river running fast enough to bring us fish, Taras, or is it just slow enough for us to catch them?"

Taras laughed.

"Luda, you're funny."

"I'm not trying to be funny! Why did you laugh at me? I've never fished much."

"It's all right, Luda. I'm not laughing at you."

Luda tugged at the line. "It feels heavy; I must have a bite."

"It feels heavy because there's a weight to take it to the bottom." Taras pulled 2 corks from his pocket.

"What are those for?" Luda held the light cork in her hand.

"If we don't catch any fish that live at the bottom, we'll try corks to keep the bait floating near the surface. Maybe there, among those fallen tree branches."

"Did Vadeem teach you that?"

"Yes, Luda."

"We really need to catch this fish, don't we, Taras? Is that why we aren't catching any?

"We aren't catching any because we're talking too much." Taras remembered Vadeem had said that to him many times.

"All right, I won't talk."

Neither of them said a word. At the end of an hour, Taras removed the weights from the lines and tied on the corks.

"Come up here near this fallen beech tree, Luda. We'll drop our lines here."

"Where's the bait?"

"Help me run this log over."

Together, they turned over a log in the edge of the water.

"See, here is our bait." Taras pointed to the grubs on the wet side of the log.

Suddenly, he screamed at her, "Luda! Get out of the water!"

Chapter 15. Snakes and Snails

"Snakes! Snake!" He yelled.

Luda ran from the shallow water onto the sandy beach.

"Where? Where is it?" Her eyes darted everywhere wildly as she jumped up and down.

"In the water, there." Taras pointed.

"Be careful, Taras!"

Taras looked for a weapon. He grabbed a long tree limb and thrust it into the water. The snake swam for it and wound its shining, black-banded body up and around it.

It slithered toward Taras, moving stealthily up the branch. He swung the branch up from the water and hurled the snake out into the river. The current swept it away. He and Luda watched, their eyes wide in amazement.

"Oh, Taras, Vadeem told me you both had seen snakes out here when you fished. I thought he was just bragging, trying to scare me. I don't want to fish anymore!"

Taras saw her shudder. "We have to try, Luda. We shouldn't waste these grubs.

Luda's eyes grew big at the grubs wiggling. "You had some other kind of bait, didn't you, besides them? She made a face and put her hands behind her back.

"It's all gone. It was the last of the dried apple pieces. Now, here, you bait yours."

He held out a fat, squirming grub to her.

Her eyes locked on it. "Do I have to?"

"Yes, Yuri would do it."

"All right, all right."

Taras saw sweat break on his sister's brow and smiled. He thought how strong she had become. He knew she didn't like hurting anything.

Finally, one hour later the live bait had attracted only one little fish.

"I can't believe we've only caught one." Luda shook her head.

"Maybe there are more people fishing now that there's no bread. We'll have to go tonight to scavenge grain."

"The railway station is further than the grain shed was."

"I hope Viktor bites anyone who tries to get near him."

"I think he will."

As they prepared to leave, Taras spied a snail on the bank.

"Luda, look, a snail. You remember what the man who brought Vadeem home said about them?'

"No, I didn't understand it."

"They think snails somehow keep your body from bloating if you're starving."

"Well, let's dig some up. My energy's almost gone."

Using the end of their fishing poles, they pushed mud aside to find the snails.

"They're so gross, Taras; they make me gag."

"I agree, very gross." Taras felt goose bumps on his back. He tossed snails into the pail with mud still on them. How in the world could you put those in your mouth?

"Grandmother and Mother know how to cook them. They eat these somewhere, Japan or France. I don't know how, but I've read about it." He searched his memory.

"FRIED, right? Not boiled. That way I couldn't see what they were. They couldn't serve them on cabbage leaves. I've seen too many worms on cabbage leaves, moving."

"Well, some places they are a delicacy, Luda. We'll have to remember that when we get them on Linden cakes or in soup."

"Uggh, uggh." They said together, and rolled on the ground, holding their stomachs.

When Luda closed her eyes, she stared screaming again. Taras thought she was remembering the snake.

Chapter 16. Poets To Siberia

"What's the matter Luda? The snake's way down river. You're all right!"

Taras tried to calm his sister. But she had gotten off that ground. She had made about five big moves and was now sitting on Viktor's back, taking deep breathes. She grew angry when her brother couldn't help laughing at her.

"Taras, you'd have screamed, too, if you had forgotten about the snake!"

"You are right, Luda. That was just the most amazing movement I've seen in a long time, your getting onto Viktor's back. If you could repeat that, you could qualify for the circus!"

"Do you think so?" Luda sounded interested in that. "Taras, look upstream, is that man losing his cart? No,…he's got it now! It was floating away. Did you see that?"

Taras nodded as he watched a villager he assumed had been fishing, too, recover control of his cart that had rolled into the stream and started floating away. He had thought it was a boat at first.

When the children presented their offering to Mother, she held the pail in front of Grandmother.

"How do you cook these?"

"Well, Maria, since this is my first time, I'd guess wash and boil them into soup.

"Help me. It needs to be ready for supper." Grandmother even made a face as she took the pail to the sink.

Soon the soup was simmering. No one remarked about how it smelled.

In the other room Taras and Luda sat by Vadeem and watched his face.

"Vadeem we love you," Taras said.

"Please come back," Luda prayed.

Their eyes moved to the wall hanging of Jesus at the Last Supper.

At supper Luda had a question for her mother. "Mother, do you think that the man who returned Vadeem to us and told us about the snails was a guardian angel?

"I don't know. I have never heard the snail story. It makes me think of the story in the Bible where the prophet spoke to a king, was it Naman? He had to wash in a certain river to get well."

The meal was very quiet after that, but all the bowls were emptied.

It took both Mother and Grandmother to get some soup into Vadeem's mouth.

One had to hold his head and shoulder upright; the other fed him. They took turns.

It was dark when the men arrived home. The first thing they did was check on Vadeem. He was still lying quietly, his eyes closed. They moved into the kitchen.

"Did you eat well at the sokolkz?' Grandmother asked them.

"We ate zatirka, flour in water."

"Yes," His father answered. His grandfather nodded. Taras thought they looked too tired to talk.

"No potatoes or tomatoes?" Mother questioned.

"No," they said.

"The officer lied?" Taras asked.

"Oh, yes!" His grandfather growled.

Father spoke up. "Taras Shevchenko wrote a poem:

"They steal our food, rob us of our treasures, plunder our land.

Will we, hopeless, die?"

Grandmother sighed. "Don't tell anyone your father is a poet." she said. "If you do they might send him to Siberia like all the other writers, or scholars, or nationals.

There they work in the mines or forests, or perish in a prison."

"Mother, do we have any coffee?" Tara asked. "I think Luda and I will need some to keep us awake the next time we make a railway run.

For the first time Mother did not say they were too young for coffee.

Chapter 17. The Railway Station

The road to the station tonight felt longer and harder to Taras than the day he came home from his uncle's house. He had been on foot that time, but he had had more hope than he did tonight. There was barely enough light to see by. No bright moon lightened the way or his heart. Also, he felt more fear of the soldiers than he had before when he was still learning about who they were and how they acted.

"How much further is it, Taras? I can't tell much. There's not enough light."

"I know, Luda. I'm sure glad Viktor sees well. They gray color of the road probably helps him."

"You're right."

"Viktor probably just thinks we're going to the village as usual."

"Probably."

Taras was glad his sister felt like talking. Maybe she wasn't as worried as he was.

He didn't know what to expect tonight. He wished he could have talked to Vadeem about how the grain was stored.

But Vadeem had yet to speak.

The village was eerily quiet and dark.

"People are sleeping more because they haven't eaten as much," he told Luda. He hoped they were sleeping. What else would explain why things were so quiet?

Only the church seemed alive as they rode past it. Lights in the stained glass windows. Laughter through the night.

Luda prayed aloud, "God help Dimitri."

"Amen," said Taras

"Let's come see him tomorrow."

"If we get grain tonight and eat in the morning," Taras answered.

Viktor had to rest more now. He wasn't eating as much. He slowed down. Taras reined him in under a tree near the closed store.

"Is it safe here, Taras?" Luda looked back at the noisy church.

"For a moment, until Viktor rests."

"Don't forget and call me Luda in front of the soldiers, Taras."

"You're right, Yuri. We're going two more streets over, and then we'll tie Viktor near the candy store. The store will be closed and dark so no one will notice him."

Noise at the church grew louder, and looking back, Luda noticed the front doors had opened. Soldiers were outside now, smoking and drinking, probably.

"Let's go, Taras."

"All right," he said, and helped her up onto Viktor's back.

In minutes Taras had given the horse a chance to drink at a side street fountain and tethered him.

=======

They crept through the tree shadows until they were hiding across from the rear of the station. The grain was piled inside fences. Taras saw a light had been rigged at the back where the fences were. There was a tarp covering some of it.

If we can crawl under the tarp without being seen, he thought, we can pack some inside our coat pockets.

The station was a good place to take back grain they had grown. It was where their grain was being out into box cars and transported out of their starving country to places he bet people weren't going hungry.

"Luda, when I run across the street in a minute, you wait a few seconds and then you follow me."

"Taras, don't leave me." His sister grabbed his hand.

"We have to across the street separately. Less chance of the guard noticing."

"All right."

Taras wished he had on a knit hat like Vadeem wore. He'd feel less exposed. But he didn't. At least his hair was dark. So he ran, crouched down, to the back of the grain compound.

A tall new board fence guarded the entire back yard of the station because the Russians had built it to house the grain they were shipping out. A wire gate connected both sides of the fence to allow entrance. The board fence was high enough to allow them more protection from the view of the soldiers, but it also allowed less chance of someone climbing over it to get at the grain. The gate provided them the best chance even though it was padlocked. He could see where some grain seeped through the wire there despite the fact that they had put a tarp over some of it. Maybe they could work quietly on the bottom of the pile at the gate.

Seconds later, Luda fell next to him, out of breath.

"Why can't I breathe, Taras?"

"I don't know. Maybe you're scared, Yuri."

"Maybe I am," she whispered.

"When I lift this tarp, crawl under."

Taras tried lifting a corner but it was too heavy.

"Yuri, help me lift it," he hissed.

Luda grabbed a corner and strained. It pulled up.

"Quick! Get under it. They're coming," Taras whispered Luda worked herself up under the tarp until she was right beside Taras.

Light from the station spotlighted the contents.

"Peas! Taras! We haven't any all year."

"Shh... he'll hear you."

Boots marched around the corner of the railway station. Taras only hoped their bodies were not outlined by the tarp.

He hardly breathed. The boots paused near them. He heard two voices.

"I thought I heard a noise, but I don't see anything."

"Neither do I, except this loose place here at the bottom of the tarp, where an animal might get in."

"What animal? The Ukrainians are eating all of those. Have you seen any cats or dogs lately?"

"No, but who can blame them. They have no bread."

"Those new soldiers had no idea people were starving here. They just thought they were supposed to make the kurkels sign their farms over."

"Right."

"If Fritz heard our sympathy for these people, he'd shoot us and the people you thought you heard."

"You're right."

"I know. Shoot at something. That way he'll think we're doing our job."

Chapter 18. "Shoot at Something"

Taras froze. He reached for Luda's hand beside his and held it. If they had to go, if would be together. A shot rang out. He thought it was in the air above them.

Luda squeezed his hand. She was all right.

The soldiers walked back around the side of the station. Amazing. Some of the Russian soldiers didn't hate them or want to see them die.

Like Boris. He wondered how Boris was. Boris had saved their lives. They hadn't told Father and Grandfather about that night. They might not have let them come back for grain.

It was been quiet for a few minutes.

"Yuri, you pack peas; I think I feel grain to the right of me. I'll pack that. Hurry!"

In a few seconds, Luda squeezed his hand. He had finished pushing grain into his pockets, too.

He started backing out from under the tarp. Hearing voices again, he stopped.

He recognized the voice. It was Fritz. He addressed the other guards.

"When do those boxcars with the dead bodies get here?"

"Couple of hours yet. They don't want them to be seen," one guard said.

"We might really have mutiny on out hands then, with people so hungry!" The other guard spoke.

"Not hardly, my friends, haven't you noticed how much in control we are?"

First and last, it was Fritz.

"Be quick! Get your tools together. While I fill out this report for the commander, you secure the tarps," Fritz ordered.

The soldiers went back into the station to gather their tools, and Fritz went to do his report.

"Let's go. NOW!" Taras whispered to Luda.

In moments the children had backed from under the tarps and run for the trees.

Just in time, too, because the soldiers had returned to the back of the station with mallets and big nails.

"Close call," he breathed to his sister and quietly tiptoed down toward the place they had tied the horse.

"Here's your reward, Viktor, for your part." He cupped his handful of grain he had pulled out of his pocket for his beloved horse and held it under his mouth.

"He wouldn't like peas, would he?"

"He's all right. Let's go before we are heard or seen."

When they were on the road, Luda nudged him. He slowed the horse.

"Taras, don't you think it would be safer to stop and see Father Dimitri now?"

"You mean while it's dark?"

"Yes, the soldiers might wonder if they see us in the daylight again."

"All right, we'll try. The soldiers seem to be inside."

They edged Viktor toward the back of the church, walking instead of trotting him.

They guided him to the back of the shed where he wouldn't be seen and tied him to a pole in the rear.

"Quiet, now," Taras spoke to Luda, "like mice."

They tapped on the door. Dimitri opened it and in the light of the lamp, they saw his eyes beam.

"Come in, children."

Inside, they hugged him and asked how he was.

"As well as any of us can be, under these conditions. Actually better than most, I fear, because they do let me eat. I feel guilty, every time I eat. At least people are coming every night to share in leftovers I can give them, like I suggested at the swamp."

"You shouldn't feel guilty, Father. If you hadn't agreed to look after things here, they'd have shipped you to Siberia. Then we wouldn't be able to see you!"

"Or worse. I've heard them say that they've killed many priests and closed many churches. It breaks my heart. They say there's no room for religion now."

"Killed priests?" Luda couldn't believe it.

Dimitri nodded. "But look I have good news for you."

A boy stepped out of the shadows. He pulled off the cap that had shaded his eyes.

"Do you recognize him?"

Taras was overjoyed! Father Dimitri is letting me stay here and help him." Alex explained.

"My family is all still missing. The soldiers came to our farm and tried to get my father to sign it over. He refused so they took us to the station and put us on the train for the work camp in Siberia. I was upset and had walked outside onto the ramp connection between the cars. I was thinking about jumping off when the train lurched and I fell off. I walked back and came here since I didn't know what to do or where to go. My family didn't escape like I did. God help them."

"Do the soldiers know you're here?" Taras wondered.

"Yes, they think I have amnesia. Dimitri said he didn't know me. He can't admit that I'm from a kurkel's family. They'd kill me or reship me to Siberia."

"Here, eat the rest of our supper. I know you're starving." Dimitri handed them a covered plate. They quickly unwrapped it and picked up pieces of bread and potato.

"Slow down, so it won't make you sick," Dimitri held up his right hand in emphasis.

Two loud knocks sounded at the door.

Dimitri motioned Alex to his cot and Taras and Luda under the table where his kitchen supplies were. He dropped the cloth covering the top of the table down over its front to hide them and answered the door.

Chapter 19. The Hunter

Taras stepped silently out of the shed, Luda close behind him. Thankfully, it was dark, but something didn't feel right. It was too quiet, too still; fear clutched at his heart.

Someone might hear them. He froze motionless, signaling Luda to do the same.

Suddenly a bright light turned on, from the back of the church. The circle of ground around them lit up as if it were daytime.

A single figure moved toward them, but the light was behind him, so they couldn't be sure who it was. Taras knew one person who moved as if he were stalking someone.

"Come out here, you idiots, NOW," the voice boomed. "I was right! See what I have caught!"

Fritz. Of course. He knew that voice. A number of men started filing out the back door of the church. At his beck and call. At the crack of a whip. He expected Boris had felt it.

"You may say that I am wrong. These may be sympathizers among you, but I want all of us to go to the train station. I will give you proof, there.

"You two boys will go in front of us, walking, not riding. And blindfolded, hands tied. That way I can keep up with you. Don't try to run. You see our rifles." Fritz made a show of attaching a clip of bullets to his own weapon.

"Father Dimitri, you stay here; we'll be back. I am sure you were in on this."

They saw Fritz's face now. The dark made him look even more menacing than the daylight. Black, flashing eyes. Dark deep furrows in his forehead. A steely, straight-lined mouth. His teeth ground when he wasn't talking.

Taras felt hate rise like bile inside him. He stepped out, almost reached for Luda's hand, then remembered Luda was Yuri, now, and no one must know she was his sister.

She moved beside him, and a soldier they didn't know tied on their blindfolds.

"Commence!"

The walk to the station began, with a soldier on either side of them to guide them.

Behind them they heard all the soldiers walking. One complained.

It's late, commandant; why don't you just tell us what you're doing, instead of making us march to the station?"

Taras paused, turned toward the voice, and listened in astonishment as he heard a shot. The soldier who had spoken? He heard a thud onto the ground.

"Any of the rest of you have questions for you commander? You should all know I don't tolerate insubordination. Boris probably knows that best."

Probably from your whip, thought Taras. You don't even tolerate a question.

All was silent except the man who had suffered the injury. He was softly moaning "my leg, my leg," into the dirt.

"We won't force you to walk, Vasyl. We'll pick you up on the way back."

The group marched silently the rest of the way to the station.

Taras believed all these men might hate Fritz. He led without respecting his own soldiers.

They arrived at the front of the station. When they were in place, the blindfolds were removed. Taras saw that it was dark except for a light at the grain enclosure.

"Wake up!" Fritz bellowed. "Come out here and see the culprits who visited our grain compound tonight and whom you did not catch. You are slovenly guards!"

Two sleepy, disheveled soldiers stumbled outside into the backyard of the station.

"Sorry, commandant, sorry; what did you say we didn't do?" One of them mumbled.

"Put some lights on the station yard. I\ll show your error! You should get a punishment like Vasyl. Who wants to tell them what Vasyl's error was?"

"He questioned the commandant's order to march over here. The commandant shot him in the leg."

The men looked at each other and rushed to do Fritz's bidding. They looked where he was pointing. He had pulled back the tarp at the gate with some of his men.

Midway up, Taras could see the outline of his and Luda's bodies, where they had lain to get the grain. Oh no, he thought. Below, he could see where they had slid back down and out from under the tarp.

"Now, do you understand why I say these two visitors of Father Dimitri's are the ones you didn't see take grain tonight? You better not have seen them, because I would not tolerate sympathizers with the Ukrainian peasants. That would be a crime as bad as taking this grain which is state property."

It will never be yours; you've just stolen it! Taras thought.

"We are ordered to shoot those who disobey that law, who take state property."

Dear God help us, prayed Taras in his head.

"Let's all go back to talk with father Dimitri and see what he knows about this."

Fritz ordered the soldier to blindfold Taras and Luda again. It seemed like a funeral march back to the church. Taras reached out and touched Luda's arm. She hadn't uttered a sound.

When they reached the backyard of the church, Taras saw the lights on in the shed. Father Dimitri and Alex stepped outside.

Fritz addressed his questions to the priest.

"What do you know about these boys taking grain, Father?"

"I know nothing about them talking grain, Commandant."

"You do know them?"

"Yes, of course, I have known them since they were babies."

"I find it strange that you don't know that they have been stealing grain."

"Well, certainly, I am not with them except for brief visits, I don't know all their activities."

"Well, maybe you should have known more. You could have counseled them to do the right thing, not to take grain. You would have saved their lives."

The right thing, thought Taras. How would he know the right thing, if he shot Vasyl for asking a question?

"Perhaps I should have counseled them."

"Not perhaps. Definitely. Do you know the law regarding theft or state property, Father?"

"There are so many new laws I can't keep up with them."

"It would pay you to keep up with them. They affect living in all sorts of ways.

Like these boys here, if you had counseled them, they might have lived longer."

"What do you mean, Commandant?"

"I mean the law now says to shoot anymore who steals state grain, which they plainly did!"

"The law says to shoot those who take grain that they grew themselves because they are starving? Is that not a very cruel law?"

Taras had never heard the priest speak so boldly. He was terrified and jerked his head downward. The blindfold shifted slightly upward on his forehead and gave him an opening. He saw black boots, directly in front of him. Fritz's?

"Old man, you are very stupid to speak to me in such a manner! You barely escaped death or deportation to Siberia. You dare question the laws our esteemed Premier has effected? I see you are no longer satisfied to polish our boots; you want to meddle in our business. You come and stand with these young thieves. You are no better!"

Taras carefully drew his right boot straight backward.

"Tonight you three die for crimes against the state. Let this action be a lesson to all of you and this village. I alone am the firing squad!"

Taras heard Fritz cock his pistol.

Immediately he launched a super kick into the bootleg in front of him. A shot rang out. Then he heard something fall.

Chapter 20. Aftermath

Taras heard a fearful groan; he pushed the blindfold off and saw Fritz on the ground.

The voices of the soldiers surrounded him.

"What?"

"Who did that?"

"Is he dead?"

"Who killed him?"

"Be still, men; stand where you are." Boris stepped forward. Was he next in command?

Boris knelt down beside Fritz and felt for a pulse in his neck.

"Your commander is dead; there is no pulse! Oleksander, you are now second in command after me. Come here and tell us what you find." Boris rose to his feet and backed away from Fritz's body.

Oleksander lowered himself beside Fritz and put his finger on Fritz's wrist, then his neck.

"There's no pulse."

Boris turned to face the men. "Who did this?" He asked. His eyes searched the churchyard.

"I knicked him in the knee," Taras answered.

"I'm asking who fired the shot?" Boris asked.

There was no answer, just a lot of shaking of heads.

Then a faint voice answered from low in the bushes. "I shot him."

Vasyl dragged his body slowly and painfully from the nearby woods into the light.

Two of his fellow officers went quickly to him and picked him up. They carried him closer by to a cot. He sat up to talk to them..

"After Fritz shot me, I crawled into the woods. I couldn't think well, and I didn't see anyone to call for help. I inched toward the church and waited."

There was complete quiet.

"I had to stop him. He was about to shoot a priest and two children." Vasyl threw up his hands in despair.

"Do what you must with me, but their lives are worth more than mine."

The men started talking between themselves.

"You wanted him dead; you hated him," one soldier said.

Another said, "Who didn't hate Fritz?"

Father Dimitri held up his hand for quiet. "Talk later. He's lost blood. Some of you take Vasyl to see a doctor. I have the address of the one in Torchanova in the church.

"Use my carriage." The priest hurried inside the church.

Taras felt Luda grab his arm for support, or out of fear. He turned to look at her.

She appeared dazed.

Boris tapped two men in the front of the group to go.

"I thank God this didn't end the way it started," he said. "We'll have to discuss with Father Dimitri where to bury Fritz."

The men nodded.

Boris stepped away from his men, stood over Fritz, bowed his head, shook it, all with no more words.

Taras felt a hand grasp his shoulder. It was Father Dimitri. He learned down to speak into Taras's ear. "You and Yuri go on home! Be careful. Your parents will be worried. I don't know what will happen next! Everyone won't agree with Boris. You are fortunate Fritz didn't check your coats for grain before he died. He would have disposed of it."

As Taras and Luda walked away from the scene where they had thought they might die, Taras felt many eyes on them, and not all of them friendly.

Chapter 21. Nadiya's Fury

"Taras." Luda had been quiet while they traveled home until now.

"Yes, Luda." He slowed Viktor to a trot so he could hear her better.

"Did you ever think you'd be thankful for something bad happening?"

"What?"

"That commander, shot."

"Fritz? Yes, he might have hurt Father Dimitri, or Boris, or us. That's the most afraid I've ever been."

"I know. I was, too, Taras. I'm relieved over a man being shot. I never thought I would feel this way about a death."

"The man was about to under three people, Luda."

"Do you know other soldiers that bad?"

"Well, yes. The one who tried to get Father and Grandfather to sign the farm over is one. Nikiforov."

"Where is he now?"

"I don't know."

Taras felt Luda tighten her grip on him.

"He sounds awful, Taras."

"He was. He ordered our friend's fathers to Siberia."

"Maybe we'll never see Alex and Sonya and Ilsa's fathers again."

She paused. "What if something happened to our father or grandfather, and we never saw them again, Taras"

"Oh, Luda, that's an awful thought. I've had it, too."

"I couldn't bear that, Taras."

Taras changed the subject. He was afraid he couldn't tell Luda what she wanted to hear.

"Are your pockets still full?"

"I think so, Taras."

Her voice quivered.

"I'll never complain about what we have to eat again."

"Neither will I, Luda." As long as we eat again, he thought.

A lot of noise to the west of the road caught their attention.

"What's that, Taras?"

"I don't know. Let's go see."

"I think it's at the farm where Father works."

Taras pulled Viktor into the woods across from the silo.

"Look, they've added another shed, Luda. Look at all the grain...they took from us. That first shed used to be ours."

Shouts filled the air. Women were shouting and screaming. Not men. It sounded like threats.

"See, up on the roof, Taras?"

"Nadyia, don't stand up there! It's a clear shot for them!"

Taras and Luda's eyes searched the roofs of the sheds. They finally found her. A woman stood on the roof of the first shed, her long, pale hair flying in the wind. She held a rifle in her right hand; she raised both her arms upright in the air.

"Nadyia, get down! They'll shoot you without warning!"

"No, I want them to see me! So what if we die one day early?" We're dying now!

"So are our children!" I'll never see them grow up. Fill your bags with grain, quickly!"

She must be the leader, Taras thought.

He really wished Vadeem were here. His brother would know what to do. There was no time. If anything could be done, they would have to do it. A distraction?

Across the road three soldiers on horseback were making a plan.

"Hold on, Luda! We're riding in." Luda grabbed his waist and Taras yelled, "Go Viktor!" They thundered into the yard, through the midst of the soldiers, knocking two down. Then they quickly disappeared into the woods and circled back to where they'd been. A storm of horses' hooves... and more soldiers arrived.

Chapter 22. The Women's Revolt

A fallen soldier yelled from the ground, "Children, … a brute, black horse attacked us!"

"It's Karpenko's yard!" One man, arriving, shouted, "Watch out! I see weapons!"

There were no guns in the other women's hands. There were pitchforks, poles, and rocks. These were their weapons. Vadeem had said they should arm themselves.

"Look at those guards, Luda; don't make any noise."

The young woman held her place fearlessly on the roof. She pointed her gun at the head guard.

"How can you keep our grain from us? We grew it. Our husbands, our fathers.

"How can you think you're right to take it from us? You're killing us! You're the worst enemy of all, the robbers of our food! Take grain, ladies, put it in your sacks. I'll protect you!"

The women surged forward. They swung axes and splintered the shed's walls.

Some of the soldiers looked as if they sympathized. Many looked confused, as if they didn't know what to do. Had they seen women ready to battle before?

Suddenly a voice called them to action.

"Stop them; that grain is the State's property!" The head guard raced forward, aimed and fired at Nadyia. She screamed and clutched her chest where a red stain began to spread. Then she toppled off the shed roof to the ground, silent and still.

Taras flinched. A new martyr. How senseless.

Nadyia's act spurred the women to fill their pails with grain. They screamed again and pushed toward the soldiers, striking them with their poles if they didn't move out of the way.

Women hurled rocks at other soldiers. One large rock struck a soldier in the temple, and he fell, unconscious. Soldiers wrested poles away from the women and used them to shove them away from the grain sheds.

"Go home! Your children will be orphans if you don't!" The soldiers yelled taunts at the women.

That strategy only succeeded in enraging the women. They hurled more rocks.

Protected the ones who were filling their buckets.

Taras suddenly punched Luda. "Isn't that our cousin, Tatiana?" He pointed at a woman in a yellow shawl at the forefront, nearer the grain shed. They still watched from the woods across the road.

"Yes," Luda hissed, "Oh, God!" They saw Tatiana fall.

The soldiers began to fire on the women who didn't stop filling their pails.

The victims began to litter the ground. Tatiana did not get up.

Some of the women were strong as men the way they fought back to get grain.

A sudden wind began to rise in the trees behind them and rustled the leaves, making it harder to hear. Taras felt cold. He pulled his jacket closer. Luda leaned into his back. Did being afraid make him this cold?

One woman begged a soldier facing her. "Please have pity on my children!"

Taras grabbed his sister's hand behind him. "Help me scream; Luda, it will distract them, "he hissed in frustration.

"AAIIEE! AAIIEE! AAIIEE! They screamed together.

Soldiers looked away from the scene as if they couldn't figure what was happening. Were there more women or men out there coming?

"AAIIEE! AAIIEE! Taras and Luda screamed agin and again. "AAIIEE!

AAIIEE!" Then Taras pitched his voice as low as it could go. "LEAVE, LEAVE, LEAVE THEM ALONE, I SAY! HEAR ME; HEAR ME! LEAVE THEM ALONE!"

A remaining soldier rallied the others. "Let's go get backups. We have to secure this grain!" It was as if he wanted no more of the killing of women. The soldiers seemed glad to follow him. they didn't look back at the bodies. Maybe they couldn't bear to see what they'd done.

Some women who had pretended to be shot, got up from the ground and finished filling their pails. Others lay where they'd fallen. Moving no more.

Others were being very quiet now as they left the scene, stumbling back toward home. Some saluted Nadyia as they passed their leader's lifeless body on the ground.

Luda and Taras suddenly realized that the grain was unguarded, at least for the moment. They slipped down from Viktor's back to get what they could carry. Two pails sat near women who were dead. They picked them up.

"Let's try to go get help for the wounded, Luda, hurry!" He swung up onto Viktor's back and helped Luda up. They galloped at full speed toward home. Taras still knew; however, that whatever they did, there would be new orphans tomorrow. Nothing could change that now.

When they got to their own yard, they were so exhausted that they half-fell off Viktor., They didn't take him to the barn, but called out to their father and grandfather for help. Father appeared at the door and didn't understand there was an emergency at first. He just looked amazed at the two pails they carried.

"How in the world did you get *buckets* of grain?" He asked them.

"It's awful; hurry, get Grandfather and harness Viktor to the cart. Go to the field where you and he work. Some women staged a revolt and got shot. You may have time to get someone left alive, back here before the soldiers return with reinforcements."

"We'll help here;" Luda offered, "we'll boil water and make some bandages."

"We have some good news, at least. Go look in the living room," Father announced as Grandfather bought the cart. "It's Vadeem; he's recovered!"

They raced in the house to see their brother.

"You were good nurse and doctor," Vadeem stood up from a chair and flexed his arm muscles. Mother and Grandmother, too."

"Vadeem, you're back; you're back!" Luda was beside herself with joy.

She and Taras surrounded their brother with hugs and smiles.

Taras looked at Vadeem in wonder. "I was so afraid we'd lost you!"

"Not a chance, I have to be around to keep you two in line!" Vadeem shook his head, his teasing smile back in place.

As the three held hands, Luda looked at her brothers. "Thank God," she said.

"I just hope Father and Grandfather get there in time; otherwise, they run the risk of being seen or heard." Seeing Luda's frightened expression, though, Taras regretted what he'd just said.

"Get where in time?" Vadeem asked.

Chapter 23. Home Hospital

Ilia and Nastya eyed warily the long metal forceps, tapestry needle, thread and whiskey that Mother and Grandmother brought to the kitchen table to do surgery on Ilia's bullet wound. Luda cut bandages from a sheet while Mother poured whiskey into the arm wound to clean it. It took three attempts for Grandmother to retrieve the bullet from Ilia's arm. Ilia yelled out twice during the searching and the sewing up process, even though she bit down on a rubber ball.

"Here's the troublemaker, my dear; you might want to keep it to remind your men folk of women's bravery in hard times, too. I'm sorry I had to hurt you. After all, I've just met you." Grandmother handed her the bullet.

Mother brought Ilia a sling she'd made from a scarf she usually wore to church.

"Use this sling to rest your arm; it will remind you to take special care of it until it heals."

She treated with the whiskey the perforation wounds on Nastya's back that a pitchfork had made. A soldier had pushed her backward into one her friend held. Three of the punctures needed stitching. During this ordeal, Nastya bit down hard on the ball and took deep breaths, too.

When the work was done, the women spoke. "We thank you and your family so much for all you have done for us. Taras and Luda came and got you, and we thank them, too." Nastya extended her hand to shake Grandmother's and Mother's hands.

"Yes, thank you, all of you," Ilia held out her left hand. "We'll never forget you kindness."

"I can help you with one tip. I haven't caught any fish lately, but you can find snails in the riverbank you can boil for broth to prevent bloating. The meat's like gristle, but the broth saved my brother's life." Taras motioned toward Vadeem.

Vadeem nodded and smiled, especially at Nastya.

"I'll remember that. Thank you, Taras." Nastya smiled back. "We have dug rotten potatoes from the ground, made pancakes from them, and cooked them in wagon wheel oil. The snails can't taste any worse than that. And we've eaten birds, mice, frogs."

Ilia admired one of the painted eggs. "It's good we have painting and woodcarving to do sometimes when we're not too tired from working on the collective farm. We are much tireder since we've had little to eat. My husband paints starving people and the churches that they're closing. One day they'll be a source of income again.

"He thinks the paintings will help to tell the truth about this famine - that men sat with Stalin around marble table in Russia and set impossible goals for Ukrainian grain production."

Vadeem was restless. "Come on, Taras, let's go to the woods and see if we can hunt for small game." Taras went with him. He knew Vadeem shouldn't go alone.

"I've always found game. I can sniff it out, right, Taras?"

Vadeem moved tiredly into the afternoon woods behind the house. Taras followed.

"Sure, Vadeem, if there's anything out here, you'll find it."

"Shh…" Vadeem motioned for Taras to join him behind two ash trees that grew crookedly out from a single trunk, enough cover. They stood motionless and silent. The white-gold sun glinted off the house's tin roof. Dokia and Viktor softly whinnied from the barn.

"Let's go deeper. Probably nothing will come this close in."

Stepping noiselessly, they walked as if they wore moccasins. Taras thought of the winter shoes his mother made two days back of sheep's wool from an old mattress.

They'd not been able to buy shoes at the village store. He was still angry about that.

He realized he'd been following Vadeem further in, with his mind on other things.

"Shh… I heard something. Vadeem pointed toward some slightly moving bushes.

A minute later, a brown snake slithered into view, then coiled up, looking at them.

Taras shuddered, remembering the huge, black one he'd slung downstream from him and Luda.

Vadeem took aim with the small pistol, fired, and the snake jerked twice and grew still

"Are we eating that? I could try it; I'm so hungry. It's skinny, though."

"Not a chance, that's a poisonous snake. See the markings. And it's skinny. When a snake is skinny, you know there's nothing to hunt or eat out here. Nothing. We might as well go back."

Vadeem sounded as discouraged as Taras felt.

Chapter 24. The Hunt

Vadeem dragged in. Taras didn't speak.

"Are you all right, Vadeem? You're so pale." Mother said what the rest were thinking.

"All of you know I can hunt. There is nothing out there! The woods are empty of the usual small game and birds. I don't know what we are going to do. Usually at this time of the year, there are at least some other wild birds flying through to other places."

Vadeem shut his eyes and shook his head.

The room was very quiet. Everyone had heard Vadeem. His story was not encouraging. And they all needed that.

"They're reducing us to cavemen," Vadeem cried. "Eating snails from the riverbank and leaves and bark from the trees. We shouldn't take this treatement! They should go to Poland and try out the farmers over there, see if they want to give up their land, or the Russian farmers. How are they doing? Do they like this collectivization?"

The frustration and anger in Vadeem's voice were what they were all feeling.

"Are all the Soviet states suffering as we are? Or are we suffering the most?

Actually, I hope no one is suffering unless it is the ones who cause us death and starvation. They should be!" Vadeem banged his hand on the table, seething, then remembered the women seated in the room and turned toward them.

"I'm sorry." He took off his cap.

Father gestured toward the women. "The women in our family have done a good job of nursing and surgery today. I am thankful your sister is also learning nursing skills by watching and doing as she observes."

"Did you say the attack was by just women? That's amazing!" Vadeem's eyebrows went up. "...but very dangerous."

"These aren't ordinary times. Our children are starving. We have to do something!" Nastya wrung her hands.

"Of course, you are right!" Vadeem considered the young woman. With admiration, Taras thought.

"Weren't any men available to help?" He asked.

"They are at the kolkhoz working. The only thing they can bring home is what they can steal." Ilia added.

Grandfather raised his hand. "We have only been able to conceal some potatoes in our overalls so far, but it's helped us a little. Of course, no one knows what they'd do if they caught us."

Father stood up. "Vadeem, you are right. What Stalin is doing is totally wrong and immoral, but he's got the whole Red army behind him. We're no match for that.

We're in a defense mode because that's all we can do now. We had no warning they would come and take away our grain. Let's talk more tomorrow. Grandfather and I should take Ilia and Nastya home so their families won't stay worried."

Vadeem offered Nastya his arm to lean on as they left. Nastya and Ilia had been very brave. Ukrainian women had really shown their strength today. He wished he believed that the effort they were all putting forth would be enough to save them.

Chapter 25. The Miller's Risk

Awake only minutes, Taras heard tapping at his door so he reluctantly dug out of the warm quilt he'd wrapped around himself like a cocoon. The morning air in the attic was chilly. At least he'd had a little sleep.

"Taras, you and I need to make a trip. Let me come in and explain." Vadeem was sounding more like himself these days. His eyes burned with an idea.

Taras opened the door wide to let his brother in and looked quizzically at him.

He rubbed his eyes, trying to wake himself. Vadeem had always been the early rise.

He sat down with his legs closed Indian-style on the bed and gestured for his brother to sit at the end of it.

"Taras, Father says we should take Viktor and the grain and go to the miller's in Torchanova. This miller allows some of what he mills to fall into a secret drawer he built under the big milling table. he is sympathetic to fellow Ukrainians who are finding nothing to eat. He gives everyone who comes more to carry home than the soldiers would allow. At most of the mills, the officials use all of the grain to meet Stalin's increase in production requirements."

"Why haven't the Red soldiers caught him?" Taras shook his head. "They're everywhere else."

"Probably the soldiers don't believe anyone would try this under their noses. They took the grindstone we used at the swamp when they saw our lights and discovered what we were doing. The lights were essential, but they gave us away." Vadeem's outstretched hands showed his frustration. "We were lucky to get away without getting shot."

"We better go right away, then, before Luda gets up. And not a word to Mother.

Since you almost died, she's been too protective of us."

"You're right. Father knows we are desperate for food, though, or he wouldn't allow this trip either. Get some clothes on and meet me out back. We won't take the cart.

That might attract attention. What can we carry the grain in?"

"Our jacket pockets... no pails. Luda and I weren't stopped because they saw nothing to search."

"Check your jacket in the closet downstairs, Vadeem. Grandmother may have put hidden pockets in that for you." He hadn't seen her sew lately. She seemed so tired.

Vadeem nodded. "At the barn, then."

After Taras drank a cup of last night's tea and ate a linden cake, he met Vadeem at the barn. He wondered if he would ever learn to like the cakes. Probably not. At least they filled an empty spot. HE missed the borscht, but the beets were gone now. They had kept Viktor alive and moving. All the more reason for him and Vadeem to make this trip.

He had missed his brother, anyway. He's was ready to go anywhere Vadeem wanted to go.

The boys met outside the barn. Viktor seemed ready to go.

"Poor Viktor. He doesn't know what it is to carry one person anymore, Vadeem."

Luda and I have been everywhere together on this horse, since all the trouble began."

Taras buried his head in the horse's mane and hugged him. "I don't know what we would have done without him."

"You mount first, Taras, ride in front."

After his brother, Vadeem swung himself up into the saddle, and they rode out into the cold morning sunshine.

Viktor's hooves beat an easy clip clop on the road.

"I fed Viktor, Taras. The last of the grain except this. He patted his jacket.

"So Grandmother fixed your pockets, Vadeem?"

"Oh, yes, you know Grandmother. She's probably done them for everyone, now."

Riding in the early morning sun was very pleasant. Taras looked at either side of the road, searching for birds or animal life. There was none to be seen.

Vadeem started humming.

First, Taras wondered how he could sing when things were so bad. He said so.

"It's enough that I survived, Taras; I didn't die! Isn't that a reaction?" Vadeem poked his brother in the ribs.

"Taras, hey, look up, there…!"

Taras looked where Vadeem was pointing. A large grey stork glided along above some distant rooftops with wide sweeps of its wings until it lit down on top of an old church belfry. The church looked abandoned. They could see the nest. The stork looked like she might be feeding baby storks.

"Just like us, Taras, looking for food. If only I had brought a gun, we could have stork for supper."

"And what if you shot the parent, wouldn't the babies starve? I could not do it!"

"They are as helpless as we are." Taras rubbed Viktor's neck.

"Well, brother, I suppose you're right. Unlike us, though, they can pluck leftover grain kernels from the fields for their young, and the soldiers won't waste bullets on them. They'll probably survive the famine."

"Is that Torchanova ahead, Vadeem?" Taras pointed to a long hillside beyond them that had no sheep or goats grazing, but a host of little homes in a line below it.

"That's it, Taras. We have a little further to go before the miller's house, though."

Viktor slowed as if tired so they turned toward a little stream running alongside the dirt road. They slid from his back and let him lead them to the brook. They watched him drink thirstily.

"Look at those cattails, Vadeem? Mother would like to paint them. Let's tell her about them?"

All at once the sound of thundering hooves came from the direction from which the had ridden. They watched as Red soldiers galloped in a group past them, seeming to notice them, but not caring.

"Do you think they're going where we are going?"

"Hard to tell. Sometimes I think they just ride through villages to flaunt their power. To scare people."

"We better ride on to the miller's. It's past the village square." Remounting Viktor, they turned back to the road.

It was a pretty town with a cobblestone square where Taras remembered Mother and Grandmother bringing their handwork to sell at a street fair. One mile the other side of the square, Vadeem pointed out the miller's house, painted cheerfully white stucco with red doors and windows frames. They rode around back to see two other people there to get grain milled. The miller was a thin man, not robust as Taras had expected. He seemed glad to see them.

"Welcome. I am Pavla. How may I help you?"

Vadeem patted his jacket pockets. "We have grain that needs grinding. My brother, also."

"Good, then, dismount, and bring it inside the barn. I can grind if for you."

Inside the boys watched carefully as grain mysterious disappeared from sight. If Taras hadn't known of the secret drawer, he wouldn't have guessed its existence. He did see a trough catch the rest of the grain that didn't fall into the hidden drawer.

The miller bagged their flour in two smaller bags and handed it to them. The boys shoved it down into their deep coat pockets. As Taras and Vadeem remounted, they heard a commotion in the street. Taras worried that it could be the soldiers they had seen earlier. Pavla motioned for them to ride out the back door into a side yard. They stopped under a huge, sprawling oak tree.

In moments they saw a group of soldiers round the house and rein their horses to stop in front of the barn. They shouted for Pavla.

"Come out; come out, Pavla! We know what you're doing now!"

Taras and Vadeem shouted from beneath the large oak to divert the soldiers.

"Come away from him! His family is contagious! Don't go near him! Don't touch him, or you will die!" They boys tried scare tactics, but the soldiers pain no mind.

One just yelled back, "Interfere, and you both will die!"

Taras supposed that was because the soldiers all had guns. Their leader directed them to drag the miller out of the barn at gunpoint. Why was that necessary? Pavla wasn't resisting.

"You've been hoarding grain for the peasants! You are under arrest!!" A commanding officer flourished his whip while he made these declarations, bringing it within inches of the miller's face.

Taras and Vadeem looked at each other, wondering who could have given Pavla up. Was it for money? An unbelievable betrayal of such a good man!

"You will go to prison for stealing the State's property!"

When the officer speaking turned back toward his men, and Taras saw his face he gasped. Taras would have known him anywhere.

Chapter 26. The Horse's Predicament

Nikiforov. Taras would have known him anywhere. He'd never forget the cruelty of this man at the collective farm meeting he'd attended with his grandfather and Father.

More ambush than meeting, at least for those poor men he sent to Siberia.

"Vadeem, don't make any unusual moves; that officer has seen me. He doesn't like our Father and Grandfather. He called them kurkels...said they were the reason collective farming wasn't successful yet."

"He's short, Taras. I'm not afraid of him."

"Yes, but you underestimate him. Besides, the soldiers are carrying weapons!"

"You're right, Taras."

When the officers carried poor Pavla away, moments later, Taras felt a surge of anger. Good, kind people were being taken away.

"Should we go anywhere else, Taras? I can't believe what we've just seen."

"We are going to talk to Father about weapons to defend ourselves."

"I'm riding with you, Vadeem, if there's somewhere else you want to go."

"There is a friend who works in the candy store on the square. We could go see him. He might could tell us what has been going on in Torchanova. Then we best go home and tell the family what we've seen. It's up this main road a ways. Father gave me some money if we see something we can buy to feed the family or Viktor."

"We can go there. We left early. It's not lunch time yet."

In fifteen minutes they had reached the candy store on the square, but a sign on the door said the store was closed and would reopen after lunch.

The brothers looked around for something to do to pass time.

A crowd was gathering on the opposite side of the square. They were circling something on the ground.

"What do you think is going on?" Vadeem asked Taras.

"Hard to tell what's on the ground. Let's go a little closer."

When the boys drew nearer, they saw a beautiful stallion lifeless on the cobblestones. Then they overhead two men talking on their right:

"I don't blame Ivan for shooting his horse. If these Red soldiers were taking the horse for the State like they said, they will have a dead horse now."

"I don't think they'll even get a dead horse today, Vasyl."

"Why?"

"Aren't you hungry?"

"You know you're right. When they're through with this inquest for a horse, we could all get a share of meat to take home."

"I'm staying until they're done, too. I have my knife."

Taras was not believing his ears. He turned to his brother.

"That's why no one has left, Vadeem. Look at their faces."

Nikiforov's man stepped to the front of the crowd.

"Who can tell us who killed this mighty stallion, the property of the State? In this village he was always used to breed more horses. The State was going to use him for that purpose, too."

Taras looked around. No one was raising his hand to report. No one.

"I find it hard to believe no one knows who did this terrible thing."

"No one knows anything," a voice said.

"Who said that? Step forward. Now."

No one moved.

Taras felt sick, looking at the dead carcass of such a beautiful animal.

"Well, then, we'll bring back the guards to watch the horse until it's buried. Our job is over unless some one whom the State would reward handsomely will tell us the story."

"Your loss, then," the officer said, "I'm away." He used the whip on his own horse and galloped off.

No sooner had he left, than it seemed fifty hands pulled knives and descended on the carcass, each cutting ferociously until someone said, "All right, move; you've had your share!"

Taras felt sick again. But he understood. It was meat, something no one had had in months.

Vadeem was silent; his eyes stared at the spectacle.

Viktor started acting restless, moving from one side to the other, as if he knew they should leave this terrible scene.

"Hey, wait 'til it's cooked!" Vadeem motioned stop with his hands at a boy holding the horse's hoof. They boy was gnawing on it. Vadeem moved toward him.

In a flash the boy pulled out a knife. It was a switchblade, now pointed at Vadeem.

Chapter 27. For the Better Good

"Leave him alone; he's not right!" A man in the crows yelled and touched his head about the boy pointing a knife at Vadeem.

Vadeem immediately backed off from trying to explain to the boy. A far as that went, there were a lot of people in the crowd eating raw meat they were so hungry. Being so hungry would make you do things you never thought you would do. He had learned that himself in the last few months.

Vadeem grabbed Taras's arm abruptly and pointed to Viktor. Viktor seemed nervous, and he wondered if the horse sensed any danger. he nodded to Vadeem, and they backed quickly away from the crowd and scrambled hurriedly into the saddle. Viktor strained against the reins, whinnying the whole while they were leaving and shaking his head from side to side.

"Help Pavla if you can. Help Pavla!" The two men yelled at them as they rode off.

They galloped a ways out of sight from the square, and then Vadeem slowed Viktor to a walk.

"Taras, I'm really worried about Pavla, too. Don't you think there's something we could do to help him? He's helped so many stay alive. I hate for us to just run for home and forget him."

Taras was quiet for a minute then thought aloud.

"We can't rescue Pavla unless he has a way to get away. He can't do it on foot."

There are two of us already on this horse. Where is another horse? What about the soldier's horse who left the square?"

"Yes, my brother! I was just thinking that. Let's overtake him."

Taras swallowed hard as his brother did an about face and pulled Viktor in the direction the soldier had ridden. Once Vadeem set out on a mission, there was no turning back. But Vadeem was right. Taras was tired of running, too. He was hungry and he was angry.

"How will we take the soldier's horse, Vadeem? He has a gun. We don't."

"I have a plan, Taras," Vadeem veered Viktor into the brush at the side of the road. As he rode underneath a tree, he broke off a sizable stick. He handed it to Taras.

"Hold this, Taras," he said. "When we catch up with the soldier, I want you to take this stick and use it like the knights used jousting sticks. Try to unseat him."

"As we come up on him, right?"

"Yes, first I'll try to grab his gun; it will be on the same side we're on. When I get it, I want you to give him a whack in the side with the stick. He should fall sideways out of the saddle. Then I'll try to switch horses to get on his horse so we can take it to Pavla."

Taras had to hold on tight to his brother as Vadeem took Viktor to top speed.

If it hadn't been for all the beets he and Luda had fed Viktor, the horse wouldn't have been able to travel this fast.

Soon they glimpsed the houses on the opposite side of the little town. They were all somewhat the same. Most of them were white, some with green shutters, others with red front doors or thatched rooves. They passed a wooden church that looked very old and crossed a bridge over a part of a river Taras thought was the Dniester. This was a more narrow part of the river than where he and Luda and Vadeem had fished.

They passed a little chapel beside the road on someone's land. It was beautiful; someone had recently put flowers in front of it. It had a beautifully carved wooden door, and there was room for one person or passerby to pray at a time.

Another stork soared in the distance. He was probably traveling home to his nest.

Taras wished for a moment they were going home. Where they were going he had no idea, but he could feel his brother's energy. He trusted him and the plan he had.

"Taras, get ready; see, there he is, up ahead. As I get the gun, jab him in the side.

That should make him fall. He won't expect it. If I can't get the gun, you try to knock him off the horse, anyway."

The soldier was moving steadily but not too fast for them to overtake him. Taras sat straighter, watching the man's back.

Viktor's hooves pounded the dirt. When they drew closer, the man turned at the noise; his face frozen in amazement. He tried to spur his horse on, but too late. Now alongside, Vadeem surprised the soldier by grabbing his gun. Then Taras stabbed his long stick at the man's side, pushing him off his mount.

"Hold on to Viktor, Taras," Vadeem yelled and grabbed the other horse's reins.

Finally the brown horse slowed down enough for them to come alongside him.

Taras felt the sudden shift of Vadeem's body as he moved to the other horse and marveled at his brother's skill. The other horse had slowed down when his rider fell off.

Taras kept Viktor moving alongside Vadeem on the brown horse until they were well down the road. When he finally felt safe glancing back, Taras saw the soldier pushing himself up from the ground, looking incredulously at them.

"Bravo, Vadeem, where did you learn to maneuver like that?"

"I stayed in the country this year while you went to the city! That's a lot of practice. Beside you were very good with that stick. Maybe he felt what his horse has been feeling when he whipped him to make him run. That's cruel."

"What do we do now?" Taras could only feel fear as they drew nearer to Nikiforov and his men.

"We follow behind them at a distance. Hopefully we can spot Pavla and when they stop, we can hide nearby until we hand off the gun and horse to him."

"If we can rescue Pavla, it's worth the risk!" Taras resolved aloud.

"Exactly, my brother. I've never taken a man's horse before, but Pavla will likely be killed, if we don't do something!"

The sun was getting lower in the west before they spotted an encampment on the left up ahead near near the river.

"See, Taras, they've dismounted. I don't know if this gun is loaded or not, but I believe a soldier would carry a loaded one. Follow me; we'll hide away from them."

Taras slowed Viktor so he could follow Vadeem into the woods nearby, down river from the soldiers. They climbed down from Viktor and stood to plan while they let the horses drink.

"We have two advantages: They don't know we've been following them. They also may see this gun, and think I'm going to use it. I plan only to defend us if necessary."

"Nikiforov is the only one I'd like to see pay. The others have to do what he says."

"Luda and I heard two of the Russian soldiers saying they were sorry our people were starving."

"I'll bet these soldiers didn't for see a lot of what would happen here, Taras.

"Can you tell which one is Nikiforov?"

"Yes, that shortest one; he will definitely have a gun."

"It will be the surprise element, again, Taras. Pavla's hands are rope-tied. You untie his hands; if you can't, cut the rope. I'll hand him the gun. We'll have the horses nearby, and we'll show him which one he can take."

"Aren't you going to wait until it's dark, and they light a fire? There's two of us and ten of them." Taras remembered he and Luda had better chances in the dark.

"You're right. We'll wait; sometimes I'm too impatient."

When it was dark, they moved in the direction of the campfire through the woods.

Pavla sat, learning against a tree. His hands were behind him, roped-tied. Nikiforov was stretched out, napping; so were the men. They'd probably washed down their food with vodka. Several snored out loud. When Taras smelled cooked venison, his blood boiled.

Vadeem touched his arm as a signal, and moved quietly forward in the tree's direction. He touched Pavla on the arm. The man started, but then turned and recognized them. Taras tried untying him, but the ropes were too tight, so he cut the rope with one slice. Vadeem handed the miller the gun. Pavla saw Vadeem point in the direction of the horse they'd brought and tied to a tree. His eyes gleamed with appreciation in the fire's light, and they saw his lips mouth a thank you. Vadeem nodded and they moved backward silently. Pavla ws waiting for them to get out of hearing before he moved.

"Let's go." Vadeem whispered to Taras. The boys stepped back quietly until they reached Viktor. They swung up into the saddle, walking him off into the night, praying the plan worked. If it did not, they might all die today. Hopefully Pavla was quiet, too.

Chapter 28. A Stick, Not A Stone

Though the brothers were out of breath from the swift ride home, they needed to warn the family.

Vadeem got out the first words. "He might follow us here if he saw who we were or recognized anything about us!"

"Who might follow you?" Grandmother asked.

"Nikiforov. He may have seen us when we freed Pavla, the miller." Taras explained.

"*You* freed him?" Father asked. "How?" He stood up.

"We don't have time to explain. He may be coming." Vadeem said.

"That's alright. Don't explain now. Get your breath." He picked up the coats.

Mother pointed at the jackets and asked, "Is there grain?"

Vadeem nodded at her, then held up his hand for them to listen. Taras shut his eyes. He knew what his brother was going to say.

"There are some things you should all know. Today we saw people in the next village eat a dead stallion lying in the street. We also heard in Torchanova that there are body sellers who raid night wagons carrying dead bodies to be buried. They sell these to starving people. Our own countrymen. They are that desperate! Stalin is reducing us to cannibals. We have to do something!"

Luda's eyes widened, and she shook her head in disbelief.

"Pretend you never left the house. I hear horses!" Mother's chin was set. She laid the coats with un-emptied pockets in the closet, closed the closet door and placed her hands on the back of the sofa to steady herself.

There were boots stomping up the front steps and then hard rapping at the door.

"Open up in there; this is the Brigade!"

Father stepped to the door to open it.

He was practically shoved backward into his own house. He held up his hands and stood out of the way, his eyebrows knit together in anger and frustration.

"Move aside! I am Commander Nikiforov. We are here to investigate whether you harbor grain or flour, peas or beets, domestic mills. what's this on your table?

Pirogues? How kind. I'll have these. You know this is a demanding job. They sent me to replace Fritz. Mmmmmmm. These are delicious, delectable. You ladies should cook for us. Fritz was incompetent and a dangerous man, always angry. That will not be allowed!"

If my mother or grandmother cooked for you, thought Taras, you would not live out the night.

He was taking their supper! His and Vadeem's. Taras's stomach growled out loud, and he watched Vadeem grit his teeth while Nikiforov shoved the pirogues into his mouth. What a monster this man was! He noticed even the other soldiers looked on hungrily. Taras could feel everyone's anger as they stood silent, watching this small but high-ranking Napoleon-like figure swagger through their house as if he owned it.

"Look in the oven for bread! He pointed his whip at one of his men. The man lowered the door of the oven and stooped to look inside.

"None here," he said.

"Reach to the back of the oven, and knock on the wall. See if there's a secret space."

The soldier did as ordered.

"No mills in there?"

"No, sir."

Taras suddenly noticed Luda had on no cap. She didn't wear one inside their home.

Dear God, how could he warn her?

The commandant was bent on finding food, grain, mills. Maybe he wouldn't notice Luda or her hair which had grown longer.

Taras saw Vadeem clutch his stomach as if it were hurting. It probably was.

"Men, get the tools out of your saddlebags. I'll bet there is hidden grain or food here someplace."

The commandant passed Luda sitting at the table. "What a shame. This beautiful hair wasted on a boy. See." He ran his hand through her hair and turned her chin to him.

"It complements the flashing eyes. You'd make quiet a woman, son. Too bad."

He looked across the room at Maria's eyes, now bright with anger.

"I see where the son gets his looks."

"And are you finished with what you came for?" His father asked in a gravelly voice, thick with anger, a voice Taras thought he'd never heard.

"Don't rush me, or you might die sooner rather than later."

"You two are slow." He pointed his whip at two other men. "Do you wait for word from me before you move to do anything?" He cracked the whip in their direction.

"Maybe you are like my horse and need to feel the whip's sting. Take your crowbars.

Check entire attic. Look under rafters, in corners, under beams. There is obviously an illegal food supply here. If you don't find it, you may go hungry tonight. Or you may end up like Boris."

What did that mean about Boris? Taras saw his men exchanging looks at that remark and then stalk up the stairs, obviously angry.

"Is it true that at your banquets you have as many as twenty types of food on your tables to eat?" Vadeem dared to ask. Taras knew he meant to shame Nikiforov with that question, but would it be taken that way?

"Yes, indeed, maybe you'd like to join our army. You look strong enough!"

Oh, Vadeem, you shouldn't have said that! He began to look around the room for something they could use as weapons.

His father's hands held a chair back tightly. His grandfather's walking stick propped against another chair. Taras moved closer to the chair where the sick was and covered it with his hand. There was a heavy pot sitting on the stove.

"Pry up those rafters and beams; look under them!" The soldiers on the upstairs open loft floor took their crowbars and began to work on the biggest beam.

Taras saw Nikiforov rise to his full height as he saw all eyes upon him.

"Men. I think we'll take this young man with us tonight." He pointed at Vadeem.

Taras saw his father's eyes go black with anger, and his hands make fists.

The threat the commander had made about Vadeem made a fire in his own face.

"He wants to go where there is more food, a future, more things to do! Why are you looking at me that way?" He said to the eyes on him. "We have to report back with something. If not food, or valuables, then a recruit will be fine!" He strutted backward and forward, very pleased with his speech. "Don't forget to look for valuables, men."

"During one stop, we took hryvnia, embroidered wedding shirts and rings for our trouble."

Without any warning there was a ferocious crack and a long groan from above.

Taras had heard it before in the forest when his father was logging. He looked up to see one end of the biggest beam beginning to let go. Quickly, he grabbed the walking stick, bounded around the table, and stabbed the point within inches of Nikiforov's face.

Startled, the commander stepped backwards. His eyes bulging wide with surprise and rage, he looked first at Taras, but then upward in alarm. It was too late to get out of the path of the massive, centuries-old tree trunk. There was a crash, and then the room was still and silent.

Taras looked down at the fallen commander in astonishment and then away.

Finally the strength of six Russian soldiers lifted the beam as if it were a coffin.

No one spoke a word. Nikiforov was dead. They all knew it. Grandfather and Father now stood on either side of Vadeem.

"Don't worry," a soldier stopped to say as they moved their commander outside to his horse. "We will tell them it was the beam. You did nothing. Many of us hated his terror brigade strikes, his cruelty."

In moments the soldiers were gone. Taras watched them ride off, Nikiforov's body tied across his saddle. There had been no more talk of taking Vadeem.

Taras turned from the doorway back to Father and Grandfather.

"What really happened? Did they cause that beam to fall on him? Did I kill him?"

Taras asked.

"David slew Goliath with a stick, not a stone." Grandfather said slowly.

"Really?"

"Evil doesn't go unpunished forever." Grandfather said and put his arm around him.

Chapter 29. The River

It was early morning. The family gathered anxiously in the barn as Father, Grandfather, and Vadeem completed the conversion of the wagon into a boat. Taras had helped seal the bottom and pried boards from the back of the barn to make the sides higher. If a soldier saw the sunlight coming through the breaks in the barn well, there'd be questions, but that was the lesser worry now.

"That was hard work," Grandfather said, rubbing his hand. He had arthritis.

"Yes, it's been a while since we did actual construction," Father said." "Usually we're repairing furniture."

Then Father turned to Taras and the rest of the family. "Are you ready? Have you made your final decision?" He asked.

Taras nodded. "We've all decided the one thing we need to carry with us from home."

They had stood inside together in a circle. Each of them had determined what was most important to take on the journey since they might not return. Mother picked her yellow and blue egg she'd painted with the gold cross. Grandmother wore the blue shawl she'd crocheted and carried their family Bible.

Luda pocketed her brightly colored nest of dolls, and Vadeem had stood his bandura by the door. Father had hidden his slim notebook of original poems in his coat pocket, and Grandfather announced he would take the geography book with maps to guide them.

"Each of us a family member is the most important thing we take," Father said.

"Yes, and Mother and I picked what mushrooms we could find. They aren't poisonous, but they have... bugs!" Luda shut her eyes had shivered.

Three hearty knocks resounded at the barn door.

Taras' stomach rolled.

"It's Boris," the voice explained.

Boris stood in the doorway, holding the reins to Dokia. Their little horse hung her head.

"I saw her with a man on the road. I sked why he had her. He said he'd found her injured and wandering. I challenged him because I didn't believe him. He finally handed me the reins, only because I'm a soldier."

Boris handed the reins to Father. Dokia stumbled when she stepped forward but didn't fall.

"Dokia HURT? Oh, no! Where?" ... Luda rushed to the horse. She sobbed when She saw deep gashes in Dokia's side, her brown fur matted. "How could somebody do this?' She wrapped her arms around Dokia's neck and held Dokia's cheek to hers.

Mother and Grandmother hurried inside to get cloth to try and stop the bleeding.

"Poor Dokia. You're such a good horse." Tara said. He rubbed the horse on her uninjured side.

By the time the women had come back, though, Dokia had collapsed, the blood pooling beside her. Luda, weeping, sat down beside her and tried to comfort her.

Taras wiped his eyes on his sleeve. He hadn't paid her much attention with all the problems they'd had lately. Viktor had taken them on all their trips. The big horse now reached down and nuzzled the little horse's face as she breathed more and more shallowly and then stopped altogether.

"I also came to warn you; I heard Anatoly, the new commandant tell his men they were coming to this house today. The soldiers want to avenge Nikiforov's death. I didn't hear what they were planning."

"We've been expecting them." Vadeem's voice was low.

"We are going to bury some relatives' remains on the way to the river." Father took a deep breath. He pointed to a burlap bag beside the wagon.

"You may not have time," Boris said, "but I did bring you bread for your trip."

He reached down into the sides of his black boots, pulled out two long flat loaves and handed them to Mother. "I could also tell the hungriest about your horse here if you want." He pointed. "Taras told me he used to daydream that this hay wagon was a boat!"

Mother took the bread and held it to her. "Thank you, Boris, for all your help."

"Thank you for all you've done; Boris, you are family." Father reached to shake Boris's hand with both of his. Grandfather followed.

"If you ever need a house after this is over, feel free to use ours." Father gripped the soldier's shoulder. "And may this little horse help others in her death as she helped us in…her life." He choked on his last words.

Boris looked at them. "That is very kind of you. You are my family as well, now."

"Did you know that Taras reminded me of my son when I saw him that first day? I had no choice but to try and help."

He opened his arms, and Taras ran forward to hug the gentle man.

"Do you have a son at home in Russia?" Father asked.

"No, he's dead, and there is no one else. I'll never go back. I'll hope someday it will be better here and you will return. Hurry, now!"

————————

Later they were finishing shoveling earth onto a shallow grave. They returned the shovels to the wagon.

"Look. There." Vadeem pointed at a cloud of dust. It looked like a small regiment was galloping toward them.

"Be calm; all we're doing is a burial." Father warned.

Anatoly was taller, stronger-looking than Commandant Nikiforov had been.

"I am Commandant Anatoly and replace Commandant Nikiforov. What have you done to your wagon?"

"We have made it sturdy. It will carry the crops better." Father spoke.

"I see. But, why are you out here, at a family cemetery?" He looked around at several graves. "It's time you should be at the collective farm."

"Yes, that's where we're headed now. We had to bury some relatives."

Commandant Anatoly looked at each face. "There are too many dying. You need to have mass burials only."

"Yes, there are too many dying." Father's face was dark, his meaning clear.

"Well, report to the other farm immediately, then. We'll look for you there." Anatoly held up his arm and signaled his men to turn around. The soldiers followed him.

"We will race straight to the river. The dust will hide us for a few minutes."

"Viktor will go quickly. Hold on!" Father took a firm grip on the reins.

"Pray, It's our only hope." His last words were lost to the sound of Viktor's thundering hooves.

Despite the wagon, they moved quickly. Viktor seemed to realize how serious this ride was.

But then Taras glanced back. "Hey, they're following us. Look! They must have seen us turn toward the river."

Father didn't hesitate. He didn't even look back. He just drove Viktor harder.

It wasn't far to the river now.

Luda gripped his arm. "They know we're trying to escape!"

Taras fingered the stag in his pocket Grandfather had made him. He had had no idea their wagon could move with this speed.

Viktor strained toward the river. Soon it came into sight on the horizon.

Taras jerked around and looked back again. Two men were trying to flag down the regiment. Boris, Dimitri? He couldn't tell. Anatoly paid no attention to them because he knew they were headed toward the river.

Shots rang out over their heads. They had reached the river bank, and it was steeper here than he remembered. Father didn't pause. Viktor surged and hauled the wagon over the edge and down into the water. More shots sounded. The boat took direction from the current and aligned itself. Father, Grandfather and Taras guided it with poles from its sides.

Soldiers shouted behind at the bank. "Stop! Stop! You are forbidden to leave!"

Taras cringed at each shot.

As the river swept along its new cargo, the voice of the commander ordered his men:

"Save your bullets! Let them go!"

The soldiers didn't believe they were bested and continued shouting at them.

"Save your shouting! They're gone! We've lost them! Head to the Farm!"

Anatoly's angry voice commanded them to turn around.

When it was night they couldn't make a stop. They had no anchor. They had to go on. The bright moon lit their way.

By the next afternoon they had eaten the mushrooms and a loaf Boris had given them. Father, Grandfather and Taras manned the boat, steering it with poles. They'd arrive at Soroky in the morning according to the maps, Grandfather said, and there, money they couldn't spend in their own village, would pay for tickets on the steamboat to America, their new home. They'd have to get Viktor on, somehow. If they had to, Taras knew they'd buy him a ticket!

They river was the only exit the Red Army had not thought to blockade.

Vadeem had ridden Viktor on the river bank alongside the boat. At first the darkness of the overhanging tree limbs had threatened to catch in their hair, and they'd felt a chill. After a day's ride, the Dniester had grown wider and deeper than where they used to fish. Now, the sun glinted off the water and felt warm to Taras's chest.

Father said they would have to avoid any rocks that bordered the bank and watch where the river changed levels or speeds to be safe. But, the huge round elms and weeping birches they passed stood proud. Taras imagined they reached out to them with protective arms, and he felt his heart swell with relief and pride. For the first time since he'd come home, he knew hope.

Luda broke the silence. "Taras, I've thought of a name for the boat. How about *Freedom?* Would that work?"

"That's the best name, Luda," Taras cried, and he sang it out, *"FREEDOM!"*

1933 Mandel Khataevitch, one of Stalin's lieutenants, leader of the grain procurement program stated: "The year was a test of our strength and their endurance. It took a famine to show who is master here. It has cost millions of lives, but the collective farm is here to stay.

Historical Background 1932-33

1. The independent farmers of the Ukraine stood as an obstacle to Stalin's collective farming and industrialization. Only 1 in 125 were Communists. They were not meeting his increasing grain quotas. Farmers were under intense government pressure to sign over their land and work for the State.

2. Where schools still operated, village teachers might get 18 kilograms of meal? 2 kilograms of groats and a kilogram of fat a month. They were expected to work after hours as activists so that children in their daytime classes often saw teachers bursting into their houses at night with the rest of the brigade to take grain that wasn't theirs.

3. Suffering inflicted on the peasantry was not just physical (the famine, or punishments for stealing grain, or refusing to sign over one's farm for collective farming).

By 1932 an estimated 1000 churches in the Ukraine known to have been closed. They were often turned into clubs or grain silos. The churches had ministered to the peasants for over a 1000 years. Suddenly the people were not only starving, they were without priests for support or churches where they held worship, wedding, christenings, prayer groups, and burial. The bells which had inspired the people in the villages and helped them celebrate on holidays or toll for funerals were taken to Russia to be melted into iron machinery or tools.

4. Religious persecution was concealed, but priests were branded as "enemies of the people." Many priests were arrested

and deported to concentration camps like the kurkels (larger farm-holders), if they didn't denounce their religion. After the churches were closed, people who tried to hold religious meetings in homes were also persecuted.

5. In addition there was a movement to crush Ukrainian national spirit. There were steps taken against Ukrainian scholars, writers, linguists, critics,, and artists. College students ended up in prison camps. Noted historian Hrushevsky was put on house arrest.

There were mass arrests of some 5,000 members of the Union for the Liberation of the Ukraine. Even blind bards who went from village to village singing national songs and reciting national poetry were arrested or suppressed. Many were reported shot.

6. At Communist meetings no mention was made of the scenes of famine and death being witnessed by the workers. The directive from Moscow was continually repeated that "the Ukraine under Moscow is a blossoming and happy land, and there is no famine within it."

7. The Soviet Press never mentioned the famine in the Ukraine but on the contrary West printed misleading propaganda about "flowering Ukraine and her great achievements in industry and collectivization."

8. In Spring '33, a collective farm near Kiev was totally changed in preparation for Herriot, the French Premier to visit it in Ukraine n his way to Moscow. A County Theatre was stripped of furniture, curtains, tablecloths. These items were taken to the farm. The cattle shed was changed into a dining room with flowers and telephones. There were full calves butchered, beer, all kinds of foods. Corpses and the starving were removed from roads. Peasants were ordered to stay indoors. Costumes, suits, dresses, shoes, hats were provided the players. It was a

big masquerade to impress Herriot and hide the real truth of the famine. The next day, everything was returned except socks and handkerchiefs, despite the peasants begging for the clothes to be left.

Herriot reported to France that there was not a single indication of famine in the Ukraine.

9. A delegation of Americans, English, and Germans came to Kharkov and witnessed much the same scene after the beggars, the dead and the dying were removed from the city. Some were marched 18 miles away and forbidden to return. The train station was cleaned up, and smart looking waitresses and public were brought in.

Once again visitors left the country, assured there was no famine.

10. As early as 1932 confidential orders were issued to shoot children stealing from railways cars in transit.

No fewer than 3,000,000 children born between 1932 and 1934 died of hunger.

Many others suffered from losing their parents who were sent to prison or work camps West with no thought of who would look after them.

11. In May of '33 one man, Panos Skirda, escaped Ukraine to buy grain in Moscow. There it could be purchased for 1/10 of the cost.

Any Ukrainians able to escape to Russia to work received lots of bread, some of which they would dry on their roofs to send to those starving back home. They set their children with switches to shoo away birds from the rooftops, (who would eat the bread.)

12. In November of 1932 Moscow enacted a law that no grain from a collective farm could be given to the peasants until the government's quota had been met. By that year Stalin

had increased his quotas by 44%. The best farm couldn't meet these numbers.

It is estimated that the total collection of grain actually secured included at least 2

million tons originally destined to feed the peasantry. Much held in reserve and stacked, rotted away (by 1933, around 30%), yet gleaners who tried to take it were shot or arrested. A theft of 10 potatoes or 10 onions might bring 10 years in prison.

Using the word "famine" was punishable by 3-5 years in prison.

13. DEAD HORSES. Ilko Hrebelsky, in the Poltova region, was supposed to hand over all the dead horses to rendering plants. Instead he allowed many hungry people to get these, wash them in the river, and cut them up for cooking and eating.

In one village young and old consumed a sick, dead horse and were shot for it by the NKVD.

At the Lebedyn Children's Center 76 children were reported shot after getting glanders from horsemeat.

14. A famous reporter of the time, Walter Duranty, received the Pulitzer Prize for his West writing in and about Russia. He lived comfortably in Moscow by courtesy of the NKVD.

He received every kind of reward from the Soviet for reporting what he was told to report instead of reporting the truth about the famine in Ukraine when it was happening, which might have saved million of lives. More than 10 years later, Duranty told the real truth.

15. The Soviet government warned all doctors not to state true cause of death on death certificates as being starvation. Instead, they stated that "a prevalent digestive ailment" was the cause. Other causes of death often listed were "weakness of old age", heart failure, and diarrhea. The true cause was hunger.

16. Two Jewish doctors, Moiser Fishman and his wife, Olga, ignored the orders of authorities about not helping the starving by admitting them to the hospital. These doctors diagnosed them ill from some other cause and slowly restored all those they could to health. The memory of these two noble individuals will long be cherished for all those they saved from the famine.

17. Between six and ten million people died from the Ukraine famine of 1932-33.

Most deaths occurred from starvation, but also disease, shooting, deportation, frigid working conditions in Siberia, suicides both by Russian soldiers and Ukrainian people, imprisonments, and children's deprivation of parents who died before they did.

18. The year 2020, marks the 88th anniversary of the 1932-33 famine, a year without food for the people of Ukraine, when food was all around them that they had grown.

SOME BASIC UKRAINIAN WORDS

yes = tak
No = ni
Thank you = proshu
Excuse me = vybachte
Hello = vitayu
Good morning = dobryy' ranok
Good afternoon = dobryy' den
Good evening = dobryy' vechir
Good night = dobranich
My name is = Yak vas svate' _____.
How are you? = Yak mayetes'?
How are things? = Yak spravv?
Good = dobre
Bad = pohano
Excuse me = vybachte
Son = syn
Daugther = dochka
Mother = maty, mama
Father = batko
I'd like = ya khochu
Breakfast = snidanok
Lunch = obid
Dinner = vecherya
Bread = khlib
Coffee = kava

Tea = chay
Water voda
Milk = moloko
Meat, pork = m'yaso
Fish = ryba
Fruit = ovochi
Potato = barabolya
Salad = salata
Cookie = pechyvo
Ice cream = morozyvo
Restaurant = restoran
School = shkola
Money = hryvnia
Bank = bank
Church = churcha